FURY OF DENIAL

COREENE CALLAHAN

1

EDINBURGH, SCOTLAND

The wind shifted, carrying the stink of city streets. The scent of garbage rotting in alleyways. The chemicals contaminating the water in half frozen gutters. The roll of smoke from fires burning in metal drums beneath highway overpasses. Even from his vantage point high in the sky, Wallaig smelled the putrefaction. The toxic swill rose to taunt him, painting a picture of a place in decline as clean air thickened into man-made smog.

Descending through the haze, he looked left to right. The urban landscape blazed like a multi-colored grid, creating a framework, allowing him to see in the dark.

Wallaig snorted. *See.* Seemed like the wrong word to use.

He couldn't *see* much of anything. His damaged retinas wouldn't let him. Not that he cared at the moment. With his dragon in full flight, his sightlessness didn't matter. Magic took the lead, drawing his particular talent to the foreground—the ability to sense energy in all things. Dead, alive, the object of interest didn't matter. If it existed—and held space in the world—he detected it before others of his kind knew it was there. A distinct advantage for any dragon warrior, but for him a necessity...and the only reason he'd flown out of the lair alone tonight.

Not the smartest move.

He could get into real trouble out here. On his own. In the dead of night one hundred and twenty miles from home with rogues in the area and no pack mates watching his six. But the honorable couldn't always be honest. Sometimes subterfuge walked hand-in-hand with doing the right thing.

Focused on a borough west of his position, he angled his wings and sliced through heavy cloud cover. Rimmed by blue, building tops came into view. Colorful energy streams converged, surrounding the neighbourhood like an iridescent rainbow, helping him distinguish animate from inanimate. A cluster of rats tucked beneath a row of dumpsters glowed yellow. The casement above their coiled tails pulsed a greyish-white. Street lamps went from dull pinpricks to glowing steel towers with dirty glass heads.

Wallaig grimaced. So much filth. Little to recommend. His nose twitched. His dragon half rebelled, urging him to turn around and fly home.

The need to heed the warning poked at him.

He hesitated mid-glide, then shook his head. Leaving a task undone wasn't an option. Not his usual MO either, so instead of copping out, Wallaig clung to his convictions and wings spread wide, aimed for the nearest rooftop. His back paws thumped down first. Blood-red scales rattled as his claws scraped along the parapet. Metal squawked a second before the beam dimpled beneath his weight. He flexed his talons, tightening his grip on the sagging roofline, and scanned the pixilated rise of tall structures against the dark horizon.

Wings tucked in tight, he crouched low and glanced over his shoulder. So far, so good. No rogues in pursuit. None of his brothers-in-arms giving chase. All in all, a good start to an already fucked up mission.

Shuffling sideways, he peered around a crumbling chimney top. He spotted the five-story walk-up three streets over. Brick facade, chipped stone trim, rusted balconies leaning in dangerous directions. Just as she'd described—a rundown shite hole in Edinburgh's west end, no need for guesswork.

With a grunt, he examined the building more closely. His gaze settled on the lone plastic chair close to the roof's edge. Huh, someone enjoyed being outside. A smoker, maybe. An idealist, perhaps, a human brave enough to sit out at night with huge dreams and even bigger plans. Dragging his gaze from the warped seat cushion, he focused on the entrance. Outlined in bright blue, the door led into the complex from the rooftop. His way in. One story down. A single staircase to navigate, a quick walk down a short corridor to leave the letters he carried on the counter in apartment seventeen.

No sweat. In and out in under five minutes. Six tops, if he took his time.

Wallaig hopped from his perch. His spiked tail lashed through cold air as he landed beside the chimney. The timbers supporting the roof groaned. Bricks cracked together, sprinkling him with stone dust, warning of an impending topple. Ignoring the threat of structural collapse, he picked his way across ancient asphalt tiles. Moss and clunks of tar peeled away, pushing between his toes as a garbage truck rumbled past on the street below. Snorting in distaste, he raised his paw to shake the debris from his claws. The black gunk stuck like barnacles to the bottom of a boat.

He curled his upper lip. Fucking disgusting and—

"Ah, hell," he grumbled, taking a closer look. "That shite's going tae stain."

Served him right. Fuck him and his soft heart. Or mayhap, the problem originated inside his idiot head. A complete lack of brain power explained a lot—like why he stood in the midst of a city he despised playing messenger for his commander's mate.

Ridiculous. His pre-dawn escapade qualified as bampot crazy. Particularly since sending a bloody email would've taken one-point-two seconds instead of the rest of his night.

But then, Elise had been persuasive.

Worried for her friend, she'd wanted to call and explain her sudden disappearance from Edinburgh. Cyprus kept telling his mate no, and Wallaig agreed with his commander's stance. Continued contact with the human world—and Elise's friend—wasn't a good idea. It was dangerous to both Elise and Dragonkind. As the newest member of the pack, Elise understood the need for secrecy, promising to cut all ties to her old life, ensuring the safety of all.

Logical argument. Sensible course of action. Nothing wrong with the dictate—other than the fact it was hurting a female he'd sworn to protect.

Wallaig shook his head. He should leave well enough alone. Ought to unfurl his wings and head for home. The balance inside the lair was good. Cyprus had claimed his mate. Elise adored him in return. Toss in the fact she loved her new life inside the Scottish pack and...absolutely. Zero question in his mind. He had no right to stick his nose in where it didn't belong. And yet, her upset didn't sit well with him.

He disliked the guilt he sensed in her. Hated that Elise believed she'd abandoned her friend. Pretty personal stuff, and something he shouldn't know. His fault from beginning to end. He never should have read the letters—the ones she wrote to make herself feel better about leaving Amantha behind without an explanation.

In his defence, he hadn't gone looking. He stumbled upon the correspondence by accident. Distracted by some new book in the library, Elise had left her letters unattended—and one half finished—in a wooden box in the middle of the coffee table. Open top. In plain view. Recipient made obvious by the 'Dear Amantha' scribbled across fancy paper. Curiosity forced his arse onto the couch. His dragon half had done the rest, helping him read the words, making each letter glow like pixels on a computer screen.

He swallowed a growl.

Goddess smite him dead with a thunder bolt.

He ought to be shot for invading her privacy. Cyprus certainly would after learning of his ill-advised trip tonight. He deserved whatever unpleasantness his commander threw his way. Another excellent reason to turn his arse around. The situation could be salvaged if he arrived home before dawn. No one would be the wiser and...

Wallaig clenched his teeth. Nay. Not going to happen. He hadn't flown this far only to back out now. He refused to abandon his plan. Elise needed closure. He could give it to her by playing errand lad tonight. So, best to get a move on. Standing around all night wasn't going to get the neat bundle of letters delivered on the sly.

Eyeing his target, he rechecked his sightline while attempting to shake the gunk off his paw one more time. No luck. Nothing budged. He was stuck with the shite—literally.

He exhaled in frustration. Lava shot from between his fangs and splashed across the rooftop. Exposed wood caught fire. Smoke swirled into a funnel fed by a ravenous orange glow. Mesmerized by the quick burn, he watched the flames grow into twin spirals before snuffing it out. Unleashing his flamethrower qualified as stupid. He might be a bit of a pyromaniac, but he refused to let the fire burn. The surrounding buildings couldn't take it. One misstep, and the whole block would burst into flames. Fun to watch. Not great to clean up. Too many humans would end up char-broiled.

Extinguishing the last ember, he leapt from one rooftop onto the next. On the third jump, he reached the building where the female lived. He landed with a soft thump. The plastic chair scuttled sideways, then tipped over, landing on a mound of dirt. Leftovers from a garden plot or...he sniffed the air...a pile of sheep dung? The second option seemed like a better guess given the stench and—

Bloody hell. What a pit.

Every time he flew south from Aberdeen, he remembered why he never wanted to do it again. The building top he stood on wasn't changing his mind. Transforming from dragon to human form, he conjured his clothes. A long-sleeved tee and his favorite jeans settled on his skin. He stomped his feet into his boots and started toward the door. Frigid wind gusts ruffled the hair at his nape. Ignoring the chill, he reached out and grabbed the handle. A quick yank. A shrill shriek of hinges. Wallaig stepped over the threshold and, footfalls banging across the landing, descended into the bowels of human society.

The smell of urine greeted him.

He wrinkled his nose. Hellfire in a hospital. What

in the god's name were human officials thinking? The odour alone screamed neglect. The rickety railing and crumbling concrete steps did the rest. No wonder Elise worried for her friend. The apartment complex should've been bulldozed decades ago. Rounding the fifth-floor landing, Wallaig stepped over a collection of used condoms. He grunted in disgust. Christ help him. Sex in a filthy stairwell. So classy...and not a place a female should be living alone.

Everything about the neighborhood screamed unsafe.

The state of disrepair backed up his theory.

Wallaig scowled. What was the female thinking? Why the hell was she living in such a shite hole? Serious questions in need of quick answers. Otherwise, he might do something stupid, like ditch the mission—along with the rules—and save Amantha from the building she lived in before the walls fell down around her.

2

Standing at her kitchen island, Amantha Leblanc plunked a lime green mixing bowl down on the butcher-block countertop. The rubber rimmed bottom landed with a thump. Stainless steel measuring spoons rattled in protest. She ignored the calamity and, with a shove, pushed the white sugar and vanilla beans to one side. She'd need those later, but right now, flour came next on her hit list.

Heavy paper crinkled as she grabbed the bag and dragged it front and center. Digging in, she dumped four cups of All Purpose into the waiting bowl. A white puff drifted up, clouding the air as she glanced at the clock hanging on the wall between the windows in her living room. The cheap plastic frame looked back at her, second hand ticking, sounding impatient in the silence.

Music would've helped quell the quiet.

She refused to put any on. Not at three in the morning. No matter how low the volume, the paper-thin walls acted like speakers, piping noise into her neighbors' apartments. Amantha huffed. So not advisable. The last time she'd unleashed iTunes (and rocked out to Brian Adams), Ronald had banged on her door. Something she never wanted to experience again. The guy freaked her out, and it wasn't just about the cowlick. The cold glint in his eyes gave her the chills. Toss in the awful vibe he threw off like pollution and...

Amantha stifled a shiver of revulsion. Total Creeps-ville. Absolutely worth avoiding, so...scratch the music. It wasn't worth the unwanted attention, no matter how much she needed a good tune to help her stay awake.

Rubbing the grit from her eyes, Amantha shook her head. She should be used to it by now. Hell, she'd signed up for early morning bake-offs. Had gone countless rounds with her professors at Le Cordon Bleu Ottawa for the privilege of sleepless nights and, oh yeah...earning top of her class as a Pastry Chef. Her mouth curved as she sorted through her measuring spoons. Surviving until graduation day had been tough, but one hundred percent worth it. Independence came in unexpected ways and different packages. For her, the dream started with getting her degree and ended with owning her own business.

So close. She was so damn close to realizing step one in her five point plan.

Brushing her bangs out of her eyes, Amantha cracked eggs into a separate bowl. Six months. One hundred and eighty days—give or take—and she'd have enough saved. Enough to invest in the right equipment. Enough to rent an empty storefront not far from the Royal Mile, next to thriving businesses and the tourist traps near Edinburgh Castle. A gold mine in the making, but first...

Amantha snuck another peek at the clock.

She needed to finish baking for her regular customers—the cafes who hired her to make fresh pastries for the coffee and croissant crowd who stopped by every morning. She'd started with one—a place called Perk Up in the business district. Now, she worked for three different places. A great boost. Better money and more time spent doing what she loved, but...

She blew out a long breath. A lot less sleep too.

Dumping the rest of the ingredients into the bowl, Amantha eyed the list stuck to the fridge with a pineapple shaped magnet. The apple, pecan and rhubarb pies were made. The brownies and cupcakes with frosted icing and extra sprinkles done. Her scones and coffee cakes sat in boxes by the front door alongside containers of croissants waiting for the delivery guy to show up. Suppressing a yawn, she refocused on the recipe in front of her.

"Muffins," she murmured. "Double batch of each."

Brushing flour from her hands, she formulated a plan of attack. Muscle memory took over. Her hands did the rest, throwing together the wet ingredients before adding it to the dry mix. She didn't have a lot of time. Just a couple of hours to get the blueberry, cranberry-walnut, apple spice, and plain old bran muffins baked. Easier said than done, and...yup. She was cutting it close tonight. Not her usual habit, but worry always screwed with her timeline. Stress piled on, making her clumsy, drawing her mind away from the task at hand, reminding her Elise was still missing.

Vanished. Disappeared. Taken. Use whatever word worked.

Nothing changed the facts.

Her best friend was gone. No explanation. No clues to follow. She'd simply walked out one evening and never returned.

Tears threatened, tightening her throat. It didn't make any sense. Elise was the most responsible person she knew. She never would have left the country without letting her know...no matter what Scotland Yard said. The insinuation made her want to hit something. Or someone—her first choice of target being Detective Inspector Ross. The guy deserved it for his lack of attention. How could he not care? How could he be so dismissive of her concerns?

With a scowl, Amantha picked up a wooden spoon. "The butthead."

Why wouldn't he do his job?

Every time she visited the station, she got the same old song and dance. The police always turned her away. None of them wanted to hear about a Canadian girl gone missing in a bad neighborhood. Especially with a serial rapist on the loose in one of the more affluent boroughs in Edinburgh. The attacks had been all over the news. In every newspaper and on-line journal in the past month too. Which pissed her off. How could Ross say, with any certainty, the creep wasn't responsible for Elise's disappearance? Amantha watched all the crime shows. Knew a thing or two about procedure and how law enforcement zeroed in on perps. So...she frowned and tossed a cup of cranberries into the muffin mix...what indicated the guy was a stay-close-to-home offender, sticking to the same area instead of hunting in different parts of the city?

"Great question." One the detective had yet to ask. With a bang, Amantha tapped her wooden spoon on the bowl edge. "Ross needs to get a clue."

A suggestion she'd made more than once to the Detective Inspector, which prompted him to shut the door in her face. Super effective, standing in a hallway arguing through a door with a man who refused to listen. Amantha huffed. The jackass and...now, it was official. Creepy neighbor living down the hall. Serial rapist on the prowl. Best friend missing, and a lazy detective who didn't give a damn.

No need to convince her. She lived smack dab in the middle of psycho central.

The realization made her want to barricade the door with heavy furniture and never leave the house. Too bad for her but staying home wasn't an option. Not today. She planned to visit Ross again. For the tenth time. Maybe this trip would be different. Maybe she'd get some answers. Maybe, if she got lucky, Ross would listen for a change and take Elise's disappearance seriously.

A long shot, but well, hope sprang eternal.

It had to, simply couldn't let her down right now. The idea of Elise being hurt—or dead in a ditch somewhere—plagued her. She couldn't sleep. Wasn't eating well either. Her stomach turned every time she tried. The only thing that made sense anymore was this— her tiny kitchen in her rundown apartment, baking for businesses that served the hustle and bustle of city streets miles from where she lived.

With a quick turn of her wrist, she checked the consistency of the batter. Just right, no lumps or bumps, which needed to change. Eye-balling it, she poured in walnuts and folded the nutty goodness into the mixture. Next up, the ice cream scoop. Palming the handle, she spooned the batter into muffin tins. As she finished the last one, the timer buzzed.

Wiping her hands on a tea towel, Amantha turned toward the double ovens. The duo qualified as a Godsend, the best of all finds while apartment hunting a year ago. The second she and Elise had seen the set up, they'd been sold. Had put down first months rent without hesitation. Forget the bad neighborhood. The sketchy characters skulking around could be avoided. The right tools couldn't. She needed the income, and double ovens provided Amantha the opportunity to take on more than one customer at a time. More savings in the long run. A faster turnaround to reach her goals. The fact the five-story walk-up wasn't far from Elise's job at the museum and—

"Merde," she whispered, her French accent thicker than usual. Amantha closed her eyes. She needed to recalibrate. Reset her brain. Erase her memory...something, anything...otherwise, the pain would never relent. "Elise, where the hell are you?"

The question echoed in the quiet, sucking the air from the room.

A lump in her throat, she slipped on her oven mitts. Covered by pictures of candy pinwheeling over bright red fabric, the pair settled on her hands like old friends—familiar, comforting, protective—as she peered through the glass doors. Perfect, golden pastries plumped up on baking sheets. Despite her heavy heart, her mouth curved in appreciation. Yup. Looked good. The chocolatines were ready to come out.

With a tug, she opened both doors at once. The scent of flaky pastry and melted chocolate rolled into the kitchen. Amantha breathed deep. Hmm, baby. She could smell that all night long and never get tired of it. Working fast, she pulled out the trays, set the load on cooling racks, and turned toward the muffins. Four tins of uncooked muffin batter went in. She closed the oven doors, ignoring the squeak of old hinges, and snatched the egg timer off the countertop. Twenty-two minutes until the next batch could go in, so onward and upward. Apple spice, here she came and—

An odd clicking sound caught her attention.

Worried about a malfunction, she glanced at the ovens. She jiggled the doors. No problem with the seals. She rechecked the temperature. All good. Everything working well, nothing to be concerned about—

The click came again.

A quiet creak followed.

Feet planted beside the island, she stood unmoving and listened. The click turned into a scratching noise. Her attention snapped toward the front door. Another creak, this one louder than the first. Her eyes narrowed. She recognized the sound. Heard it every time she stopped to unlock her door. Covered by carpet and warped by time, the floor dipped in the hallway in front her apartment, squeaking every time someone approached her door. So, either she was hearing things or—

The door knob turned.

She watched it rotate one way, then the other. Shock morphed into horror. Someone stood out in the hallway, trying to enter her apartment. At three in the freaking morning. Alarm bells rang inside her head. As the clamour got going, Amantha struggled to rein in her fear. One hand pressed to her chest, she played tug-of-war with her intellect. *Calm down. Stay quiet. Think...think...think.* No need to panic. Whoever stood out there wouldn't get inside. Double deadbolts would ensure it. Those suckers were strong. Industrial sized. The best of the best. She'd ordered the new locks before moving in. Had watched as the locksmith tested each one multiple times.

The handle turned again.

The top deadbolt flipped open.

The snick made her breath hitch. Her heart took the hint and picked up a beat, pounding against the inside of her breastbone. An awful metallic taste invaded her mouth. Amantha shook her head. No way. Not possible. No one but her and Elise had keys and…

Amantha blinked.

"Merde de Dieu," she whispered, an idea sparking to life. "Elise."

Why hadn't she thought of that before? Maybe her friend was home. Finally. After a month of being only God knew where. Maybe, she'd been wrong, and Ross right. Hope tightened its grip, shoving fear aside for a second. God be merciful. She was going to kill her best friend. She was going to skewer, then skin her for—

The second deadbolt scraped against metal, getting stuck halfway through the turn.

A soft curse drifted into the apartment from the hallway.

About to step around the island, Amantha came to a sudden stop. Her heart sank. A male voice. Deep, gravel-filled and…she swallowed…infused with a healthy dose of what sounded like anger. Definitely not Elise. And in no way friendly.

Panic skittered down her spine. What the hell was she going to do? Glancing over her shoulder, she eyed the narrow corridor exiting the kitchen. Two choices —hide under her bed and pray he went away or give the fire escape a try. Neither idea seemed safe. Cowering under furniture wasn't her style. Neither was spending five minutes she didn't have fighting with the window in her bedroom. The stupid thing always got stuck when she tried to open it. And the fire exit? Amantha cringed. No way would she make it down that thing alive. The rusty structure with weather-eaten stairs barely clung to the side of the building as it was, add weight and whoever stood on it would fall five stories, only to go splat on the sidewalk.

The door jolted as the intruder pulled up on the handle. The shift ended the stalemate as the second bolt unlocked in a slow swivel.

Gaze glued to the door, Amantha snatched the marble rolling pin off the countertop. She backed up a step. And then another, trying to be quiet. Option three sprang to mind. Air left her lungs in a rush. Holy hatpins—her cell phone. She needed to get to her phone and call the police. Right now, before the intruder-maybe-rapist broke in and she lost her chance. Clutching her weapon, she scanned the living room, trying to remember where she'd dropped her purse. Not hanging on the coat rack. Not on the end table next to the door. Her eyes tracked to the purple love seat and...thank God. A brown leather strap peaked out from behind the backrest.

Tarnished brass hinges groaned as the door started to open.

Fear carried her forward, around the kitchen island into the living room. A large shadow fell across the carpet as light from the hallway illuminated her intruder from behind and...goddamn him along with the apartment layout. Sitting adjacent to the entrance, the love seat less sat than six feet from the front door. Now, it was too late. She'd never make it to her purse without him seeing her. And given the size of the shadow he cast, she refused to be within striking distance when he stepped over the threshold.

Abandoning the idea of reaching her phone, Amantha veered left and slid in behind the door. The heavy wood panel swung all the way open. A man came into view. A death grip on the marble rolling pin, she focused on the back of his head.

Tall guy. Dark red hair. An excellent target.

Muscles quaking, she raised her weapon and,

holding her breath, waited. She needed a clear shot. If she missed on the first try, she wouldn't get a second. The width of his shoulders told her all she needed to know: he was strong. Much stronger than her. Which meant, if he got a hold of her, there would be no need to call the police. She'd already be dead.

3

Boots planted on beat-up carpet in the hallway, Wallaig paused outside the door. Apartment Seventeen, plastic numbers hanging off wood that had seen better days. Jesus. If he hadn't labeled it a shithole before, the inside of the building confirmed it. With a grunt of disgust, he conjured a pair of sunglasses. The LEDs in the corridor were killing him. The illumination bled from multiple wall sconces, combining with trace energy, hampering his ability to detect the colourful streams.

Wallaig scowled. Sometimes he hated human ingenuity. The new-fangled, bright-as-hell light bulbs always gave him a headache.

Needing relief, he slid on the wraparounds. Fed by magic, his vision warped. As colorful energy streams normalized, the ache between his temples moved to the back of his skull, downgrading from pounding thump to annoying throb. Thank God. He didn't need the distraction. Not while he stood in a strange building fighting with the feeling something was about to go wrong.

Paranoia? Probably, but no matter how many times he told his dragon half to settle down, the beast refused to listen. The bastard turned up the heat instead, setting him on edge, making his skin prickle in warning. A chill skated up his spine. Stifling a shiver, Wallaig rubbed the nape of his neck. Something was off. Not by much—perhaps, just a touch left of center —but enough to make him wonder what stood on the other side of the door.

Eyes narrowed on the wooden panel, Wallaig fired up his magic. His sonar pinged, casting a wide net. A series of pings echoed inside his head and... told him nothing. Zero information. Zero reason to be concerned. Nothing but clear skies outside overlooking a bunch of sleeping humans inside.

Which made no sense. If a threat existed, he should be able to detect it.

Frowning, Wallaig disengaged the top lock with his mind. A snick sounded through the quiet as he flipped the second deadbolt, then waited. For what? He didn't know. Trouble, maybe, but...shite. He couldn't put his finger on it. Couldn't quite figure out what bothered him about the building or the apartment he planned to enter.

Curiosity made him reach out. His hand closed on the knob. With a quick turn of the handle, he pushed the door open. Old hinges squeaked. The sound raised the fine hairs on his nape. Closing his eyes, he hunted for the problem. Not a scent or a sound. No voices in the hallway behind him. No movement from inside the apartments on this floor or the one below. And yet...

A strange hum hung in the air, supercharging his senses, setting his teeth on edge.

Flexing his hands, he tried to isolate the frequency. Luxurious threads of bio-energy danced across his skin. Wallaig growled as delight sparked inside his veins. Hmm, yum. Fucking delicious and...he titled his head to a better read...definitely an unknown. Something different. A whole new classification. Not so much a buzzing thrum. More of a sizzle, as though electrostatic current bled through the thin walls, drugging him with sensation, seducing him with inferno-like heat, urging him to locate the source.

A dangerous path. Particularly for him.

He never charged into a situation without knowing what lay ahead first. Dragons died that way all the time. But as the abundant energy swamped him, Wallaig took an involuntary step forward. God, so good. It was so bloody good and—

He should ignore it. Should turn the hell around and sprint in the opposite direction. A smart move. The best play, all things considered, but...

Wallaig stifled a groan as the bio-energy throttled into dangerous levels. Like a siren's song, the signal sang to him, promising decadence, luring him into dangerous waters and...aw, man. Not good. He hadn't fed in a while. No time in recent months. Little inclination to find a female and draw what he needed to stay healthy either. But as another wave of energy hammered him, the hunger he hadn't felt in months hit him like a tsunami.

He groaned. Fucking hell. What folly. He knew better than to leave it this long. Now, he was screwed, a slave to his dragon half as ravenous need collided with unholy impulse.

Fixated on the open door, his beast snarled. Clinging to his control by a thread, Wallaig locked his knees. He needed to calm down. No way could he step over the threshold while riding the razor's edge and... Goddess give him strength. What the hell was it? As soon as the question entered his mind, he dismissed it.

Whatever stood in the apartment didn't feel like a *what*. Which meant it must be a *who*. His brows collided. Or rather a *she*—a full blooded HE female with—

Another blast of bio-energy rolled over him.

His thoughts splintered as need ramped into uncontrollable lust.

"Bloody hell," he muttered, stifling another groan.

Jesus help him. He wanted some of that. A piece of her. Right now.

A bad idea. Nowhere near advisable. Touching her wouldn't end well. Not while amped up by hunger and desperate need. His beast wouldn't be gentle. He was too far gone. Was being dragged inch by precarious inch toward primal need by biological imperative. Animal instinct reigned supreme, which meant his dragon would take what it wanted: fast, furious, glorious pleasure without a thought to the consequences.

Fear of hurting her forced him to drop mental anchors. Time to abandon ship. Jump overboard...whatever. Just as long as he turned the hell around and walked away.

Great plan. Perfect, but for one problem.

His dragon half refused to heed the all-halt. The bastard was already in motion, pushing the door all the way open, picking up his feet, propelling him over the threshold. Right into the siren's den.

4

The second the guy cleared the door, Amantha abandoned her spot behind it. Hiding wasn't an option. If he looked to his right, he'd see her, and she'd be neck deep in trouble. Not exactly a confidence builder, but...she drew in a shaky breath. A plan was better than no plan. It certainly beat the alternative. Anything would be better than being held down and—

She cut the thought off before an image formed in her mind's eye.

Amantha shook her head, refusing to imagine the horrible possibilities. No sense hopping down that rabbit hole. She had enough problems, and right now, staying on task would get her further than freaking out.

Up on the balls of her feet, she sidestepped the floorboard that always creaked and slid to her right. Quiet and sneaky. Quick and precise. Stealth would save her life. Making noise—blowing her chance to blindside him—wouldn't get her anything but hurt.

Trembling inside, she moved into position. He was still looking left, away from her, examining the far end of the living room. But she wasn't fooled. It wouldn't take him long to finish his inspection and pivot in her direction. The instant he did, she'd be in plain view, smack dab in the middle of his sights.

Knuckles aching from her grip on her weapon, she raised the rolling pin. Her sweaty palms slipped on the marble roller. Panic set in. Amantha pushed it aside and re-established her grip. Now or never. Everything hinged on the next couple of seconds. She refused to lose control, not when she held the advantage and—

His boots rasped against the welcome mat as he turned her way.

Gritting her teeth, she swung the rolling pin. Her target—his temple. Her aim—in no way close to accurate. Amantha knew it the moment her elbows unlocked and her make-shift weapon slashed through the air.

Too low. Way too low.

"Pull up, you fool...pull up!" her inner Ninja cried.

With a gasp, she tried to correct the trajectory. Her arms jerked mid-swing. He cursed as marble bounced off his shoulder and— *câlice de tabarnak.* She should've played more baseball as a kid. Either that, or grown six more inches. Being born male would've helped too. The freaking guy was huge. Beyond monstrous in the size department, and as he spun to face her, Amantha froze in place. Her skin prickled, but she didn't feel it. Her heart pounded, but she didn't hear it. She couldn't hear anything. She couldn't think or breathe...or make sense of who stood in her home. Couldn't do anything but stare up at him in horror.

Details filtered through the terror.

Angular cheekbones. A strong jaw covered in ginger stubble. Thick eyebrows drawn into a scowl. Long hair tied against his nape. Sunglasses hid his eyes and...*merde de dieu.* He was handsome. The realization made everything seem so much worse. Good looking guys weren't supposed to be rapists. The thought whirled like jagged glass through her mind, ripping up mental terrain, leaving her unmoored. Even as she drifted, she knew it was an idiotic conclusion. Completely illogical. Looks had nothing to do with a guy being a soulless sociopath.

The thought should've got her moving. Made her run. Caused her to scream the walls down and alert the entire neighbourhood. But as he stared at her slack-jawed, something close to awe on his face, she didn't do a thing. She was paralyzed, on lockdown, so afraid her body refused to obey the instructions her brain kept yelling. *Run. Hide. Kick him in the balls...right now!*

All great suggestions. Too bad she couldn't heed a single one.

Paralyzing fear made a pit stop inside her head. She'd always thought it a stupid excuse. Nothing but a cop out. Just something people said when cornered in an interview, a way to explain why they hadn't screamed—or fought—when faced with eminent danger. Well, she knew better now. Delayed reactions in scary situations existed in the real world and, sad to say but proof positive for the theory appeared to be her.

Nothing else explained the fact she was acting like a piece of statuary.

Too bad she couldn't say the same of him.

Despite the momentary hesitation on his part, he was fully functional now...and one hundred percent focused on her. Without taking his gaze off her, he flicked the door closed behind him. Wood thumped against wood, rattling the handle, sounding ominous in the silence as he stepped toward her.

Raising the rolling pin, she pointed it at him. Her body started to listen, allowing her to slide backward on bare feet. She bumped into the loveseat, losing her balance for a moment.

He reached out.

She bared her teeth. "Stay back!"

Her voice stopped him mid-stride. Head titled to one side, he considered her a moment.

"I m-mean it." Her voice cracked. Amantha cringed. Fantastic. Just great. She sounded a million times weaker than a wuss, about as convincing as a dead fish. "Don't move."

"Lass," he said, his tone so guttural it registered as a growl.

The threatening sound unlocked her lungs. Sucking in a breath, she retreated, sidestepping an end table. "Leave."

"I'm sorry, *kazlita*. I dinnae mean to frighten you. I thought you'd be asleep. Wasn't supposed to see you at all," he said, sounding so sincere she wanted to drop-kick him into the hallway...through the goddamn door. Not the smartest impulse. Particularly since hitting him would require getting close enough to nail him. Flexing his hands, he shifted toward her. "I know I shouldn't be here. I should turn around and go home, but I cannae leave now."

"Yes, you can. The door is right there. Turn your ass around and use it."

His expression changed, softening a fraction.

She sucked in a shaky breath. God keep her safe. Was that regret on his face? Was she reading him right? Hope sparked, making her hands tremble. Her guard dropped. Not by a lot. Less than an inch, just enough for to her see over top of the rolling pin. Strange, but...yeah. Whatever he felt looked a lot like regret. Maybe, even shame. He might be standing in her apartment uninvited, but he wasn't comfortable. And also....

Amantha took a closer look. All right, so the vibe he threw off leaned toward lethal, but nothing about him said mean. An odd conclusion to draw given the sheer size of him, but something made her think he might not be a danger to her. How she knew that, Amantha couldn't say. Instinct, maybe. Sheer madness explained her reaction too, but as she held his gaze, trying to see through his sunglasses, she wondered. Maybe the guy owned a conscience. Maybe what she saw on his face meant he was about to—

"'Tis too late for retreat, lass. My dragon willnae allow it." Rolling his shoulders, he stepped off the welcome mat. His boots thumped down, sounding like thunder on wooden floorboards. "I'm too hungry, and you're...God, your energy...it's gorgeous. So powerful and—"

"Get out." Panic closed her throat. She tightened her grip on the rolling pin. "Right now."

"Donnae be scared, Amantha. You'll come to no harm by my hand. Shite, I willnae even touch you," he said, pausing a beat. "Unless you allow it."

Surprise thumped on her. She shoved it aside. *Unless she allowed it?* The guy must be insane. "And what —I'm just supposed to take your word for it?"

"Aye."

She opened her mouth to tell him off, then closed it again. "You know my name."

One corner of his mouth curved up. "Amantha Marie Leblanc. Formerly of Quebec City. I like your accent, lass."

"You like my...you like my..." Unable to finish the

thought, she stopped sputtering and frowned at him. "Who are you?"

"Wallaig. A friend of Elise's."

"Seriously?"

He nodded.

Joy grabbed hold of her heart, making it hard to breathe. "You've seen her?"

"Aye. I see her every day."

"Is she okay?"

"Better than okay. She's married," he said, as though marriage was God's answer to every ailment in Edinburgh. Reaching beneath his leather jacket, he pulled something from the waistband of his jeans. Envelopes bundled together with a yellow ribbon made an appearance in his hand. Gaze riveted to her, he set the package down on the coffee table. "For you, lass."

She swallowed past the lump in her throat. "What is it?"

"Letters," he said. "From Elise to you."

Her mouth moved, but no sound came out.

"Your shock is showing, Amantha."

"Can you blame me?"

His mouth curved. Crinkles formed at the corners of his eyes behind his sunglasses as he shifted focus and looked over her head. "Are those croissants?"

Amantha blinked. Croissants? What in God's name was he talking about? He helped her answer the question by pointing toward the kitchen.

She risked a quick glance over her shoulder. The pastry cooling on baking racks caught her attention. "Chocolatines."

"What's that?"

"Croissants with a kick. Each one has dark chocolate inside."

He made an odd rumbling sound. "May I have some?"

"Ah..." Weapon dipping to half-mast, she watched him skirt the loveseat and walk into her kitchen. "Okay."

Rounding the island, Wallaig snagged a Chocolatine off one of the trays. He shoved half in his mouth and moaned in delight. "Do you have any tea?"

Dumbfounded, she stared at the stranger in her kitchen. "What?"

"Tea, *kazlita*," he said, managing to sound normal with his mouth full of pastry. "Earl Grey would be good."

"Are you planning to stay awhile?"

With a shrug, he flipped open one of her cupboard doors.

She scowled as he began rummaging through the shelves. "Sure. No problem. Just make yourself right at home."

"Sarcasm suits you, lass."

Well, she was sure glad something did. Lord knew the conversation didn't suit her at all. Not for the first time, she wondered what the hell was going on. Her gaze drifted to the letters on the coffee table. Shuffling sideways, Amantha transferred the rolling pin into her left hand and picked up the ribbon wrapped bundle with the other. God. Letters. For her. Tears pricked the corners of her eyes. Elise had written her. Was no doubt trying to explain her sudden disappearance.

The idea warmed her heart. Her best friend hadn't abandoned her. Not completely and—

A cabinet door banged.

Hugging the letters to her chest, she returned her attention to Wallaig. Busy searching through her stuff, he stood with his back to her. Wide shoulders taking up too much space. Long legs hidden behind the island. Huge hands gentle as he picked up a container of paper muffin cups, then put it back. Watching him, she shook her head. Strange—could be all kinds of crazy—but even without reading the letters, she believed his story.

He wasn't a rapist. Hadn't broken in to attack her. Had absolutely no intention of hurting her at all.

The idea he might be trustworthy made her wonder when she'd lost her mind. Talk about a bizarre situation. The strangest of which stood in her kitchen, examining boxes of tea. And as she watched him fill the kettle and find two mugs, she didn't know what to do—try to kick Wallaig out again...or start asking the questions she desperately needed answered.

5

Wings angled into a downdraft, Grizgunn circled above the police station on St. Leonard's Lane. Frigid air played with the tips of his twin tails, rattling venomous spikes. The noisy rush expanded inside the invisibility spell he wore like a winter cloak, keeping him hidden from human eyes. With a murmur, he shutdown the rattle'n bang and, banking left, completed another slow revolution. His magic sparked, shimmering in his veins, causing his gaze to glow as he searched the building below.

The aerial view was nothing special. Boring brick structure with a pitched roof. Wide sidewalks out front, no trees hanging over the black-topped avenues. Scanning the layout, he looked for a safe place to land. Two main entrances caught his attention: one street side, the other exited into a parking lot at the rear of the complex. He pursed his lips and considered. Lots of foot traffic. More than he expected to see so late at night.

Like ants at manual labor, unformed officers walked in and out of the human HQ. A few climbed into marked cruisers. Others hopped into motorcycles, no doubt heading out on patrol. He frowned. Or whatever the hell human police did to occupy their time. He frowned. Not that he cared. He hadn't flown into town to socialize. Far from it. He'd rather kill a human than talk to one but some things couldn't be avoided.

Not if he wanted to retrieve what he needed to defeat Cyprus.

He could see it in his mind's eye. Every detail. Every contour. Could picture the outer skin of the case along with the braided leather handle. The satchel belonged to the female he'd taken, but failed to keep. She'd dropped it in the cathedral before he attacked. The memory played like a movie inside his head: the bang of her case against stone tiles, her horror at seeing the priest laying prone, dying on the church floor. Her scream as he'd grabbed her by the throat. The hum of her bio-energy blazing against his skin and—

Hmm, baby. He could still feel it. Felt the buzz. Relived the powerful surge of her energy as terror kicked in. She'd fought like a wildcat, clawing at his arms—at his face—before he'd shifted into dragon form and flown away with her.

Grizgunn shivered in pleasure. Such a glorious moment. One he yearned to repeat, but first, he must infiltrate the police evidence locker. He needed her briefcase. The contents of the kit would contain her personal information. Her name. An address. A phone number. Humans were odd that way. The idiots liked to label things, marking their belongings in the same way dogs peed on trees. Names everywhere and on everything. At least he hoped the female had followed tradition and been that stupid.

His whole plan hinged on locating her.

Or rather the identification tag he prayed hung from the handle of the case.

Her name didn't interest him. He didn't give a damn what she called herself. He wanted her address. The second he knew where she lived—where she slept—the hunt would begin. His strategy was simple: find and recapture her. Use her to force his enemy out of the shadows and into the open. A brilliant plan. Perfect, really...but only if Cyprus hadn't kept her as a prized pet.

The thought set his fangs on edge.

His eyes narrowed on the rear entrance of the police station. Fucking pretender. Selfish bastard. The male had stolen his birthright by seizing control of the Scottish pack. Now, he sat where Grizgunn should be—at the top of the food chain...in the seat meant for him. So, yeah, the possibility Cyprus sheltered the HE female pissed him off. Made him want to unleash his venomous exhale and suffocate a whole city block.

An idea with merit. Too bad he didn't have time for amusement tonight. Not while his entire crew flew in his wake, awaiting his next command.

Firing up mind-speak, he pinged his XO. *"Hakon."*

"Yeah?"

"Is the perimeter set?"

"Six warriors deep." Black red-tipped scales flashing in the moon glow, Hakon flew in behind him. *"You want me with you—or on the north side?"*

"With me. I don't trust myself not to kill humans in there."

Hakon chuckled. *"Clean in. Clean out. No blood on the floor."*

"Exactly. I don't want the idiots to be aware of our presence."

"*Safer that way,*" his friend said, amusement in his voice.

No question. Grizgunn sighed. Sometimes being responsible sucked. "*Stay alert. Stay cloaked. I don't want any surprises.*"

"*Uh-huh. The back parking lot?*"

"*Yeah.*"

Gaze moving over parked cars, Grizgunn folded his wings. His gaze narrowed on a clear spot near the back of the lot. Less cars to avoid. More room to land. Always a good thing given his wing span. Bitter cold rushed over his scales as he dropped through smog filled sky. Seconds before he hit the ground, he unfurled his wings. The webbing caught air. His paws touched down without making a sound. Sharp claws scraping over asphalt, he searched the entryway. All quiet now. No one coming in or out. Perfect for the hunt and a well-planned heist.

Tightening the invisibility spell, he unleashed magic. His skin tingled as his body transformed, shifting him from dragon to human. Conjuring his clothes, he sidestepped crumpled soda can and glanced over his shoulder.

Hakon landed on a patch of grass. Individual blades bent, crackling beneath his paws as the big male flapped his wings. The blowback kicked up a dust storm. The contents in half frozen puddles flew into the air, mixing with sand and small stones, then blew across the lot to assault parked cars with slushy water.

As rock pinged off steel, Grizgunn wiped a droplet off his face. "Jesus, Hakon."

"Apologies," he said, not sounding sorry at all.

He threw his friend an annoyed look. "*Shift, already. I don't have time to screw around.*"

With a grunt, his XO obeyed. Black red-tipped scales morphed into human skin a second before his warrior covered up with jeans and a t-shirt.

"We'll go in through the rear entrance." Already halfway across the lot, Grizgunn sidestepped a concert barricade and walked between two cruisers. *"From there it's a straight shot down the stairs to the evidence locker."*

"You know the layout?" Hakon asked, shrugging into a wool trench-coat.

"Got the plans on-line."

"Smart."

"Necessary. I want to be at the female's home before dawn."

"Careful, commander." Grey eyes intent, Hakon treated him to a searching look. *"Impatience breeds problems."*

Grizgunn didn't answer. He didn't need the reminder. Or want to address his warrior's concern. He'd already learned his lesson. Knew all about the folly of moving on a target too soon. His sire's misfortune had taught him well. No way would he make the same mistakes. But time was of the essence. He needed to find her before the sun rose. Hesitation wasn't an option. Not when dealing with scum like Cyprus.

The thought propelled him toward the concrete pad fronting the rear entrance.

Framed by steel and painted blue, tall windows flanked doors. Boots thumping across concrete, he crossed the landing and, reaching out, yanked one open. A quick scan of the interior made him veer left toward the staircase. He heard Hakon enter the building behind him. Trusting his friend to follow, Grizgunn jogged down the stairs. One floor down he found what he needed—a glassed in reception area with a countertop and a shitload of security. To the left of the enclosure stood a door with a keypad and high tech camera. Not bad. The monitoring system was top of the line. One problem with the set up—the human behind the glass.

Without breaking stride, he unleashed his magic. Venomous heat hissed as it slithered through the air. The male-in-charge of the evidence locker jerked, then went glassy eyed. He wobbled, threatening to toppled out of his chair.

Grizgunn steadied the idiot, exerting his control. He shook his head. So simpleminded. The human race was so easy to manipulate. Snorting in disgust, he issued a mental command. *"Open the door. Let me in."*

The male didn't hesitate. He pressed a button.

A loud buzz filled the air.

The locks disengaged. And just like that, he was through. On the other side of the door. Behind the counter. Inside the glass enclosure, accessing the computer inventory files as the human sat unmoving, a blank look on his face.

Closing the door behind him, Hakon halted beside him. *"Well?"*

"Row K, number 32."

"Let's go."

Grizgunn nodded and, clearing the computer screen, followed his friend into the back room. Row upon row of tall mental bookcases stood side by side. Boxes sat shoulder-to-shoulder on each shelf. Reading the letter on the end of each row, he paused at the tall shelf marked K, then turned into the aisle. Eyes on the numbered boxes, he walked until he located the right box. Hope riding high, he grabbed the handle hole and pulled the evidence from its resting place. With a flip, Grizgunn flicked the lid off and peered inside.

His mouth curved. There it was, the plastic case sitting like a gift inside the cardboard container. He checked the handle. No name tag. Gritting his teeth, he shifted the briefcase to one side. A sticker came into view. Shiny black background. Gold typeset and...

"Got it."

"Where does she live?"

"West end," he said, rattling off the address.

Hakon grunted. "A short flight away."

"Less than five minutes." So close. Hardly any distance at all.

Grizgunn growled, satisfaction making his pulse thrum and excitement kicked low in his belly. The blood-rush turned him down the aisle toward the door. Time to go. Soon. Very, very soon, he'd have what he needed. What he'd dreamed about for years —an HE female under his control, and the commander of the Scottish pack in his claws.

Tea mug in hand, Wallaig leaned against the kitchen counter and watched the female from across the room. Without taking his eyes off her, he reached for another chocolatine, his fifth in less than ten minutes. Flaky pastry melted in his mouth. Rich chocolate did the same, making him hum in enjoyment as Amantha shifted in her chair, set one letter aside, and picked up another. Haloed by lamp light, legs curled beneath her, she frowned at something on the page and shook her head.

Downing the rest of his pasty, he catalogued her movements. Amantha was a treat to watch. So animated. So pretty. So goddamn appealing. She smoothed out the letter she held, flattening out the creases. The graceful turn of her hands caught his attention. His gaze jumped to her face. He absorbed every detail like a starving male kept away from a feast too long. Oblivious to his rapt focus, she stripped the elastic from her hair and retied her ponytail. She was a study in contradictions. Calm on the outside, heavy heart on the inside as she tried to understand her friend's explanation.

It wasn't going well. Not by a long shot.

Most males wouldn't be able to see it—her struggle, the quiet desperation as she devoured the words on each page. He wasn't that clueless. Amantha might look calm but her bio-energy said something else. True, he couldn't see her in the usual way. His damaged eyes wouldn't let him, but the shortcoming didn't matter. Not when it came to her. Strange in many ways. He didn't know the color of her hair. Couldn't see the hue of her skin or the length of her eyelashes, and yet, he saw her clearly. Read her like an open book and knew what lurked beneath her surface.

Like a supernova, her aura flamed a deep, gorgeous red. Amber tangled with the crimson, adding spice to the lure of her bio-energy. The intensity entranced him, making it impossible for him to look away. And no wonder. Plugged into the Meridian, Amantha drew energy straight from the source of all living things. She was power personified. Every Dragonkind male's dream come true. Temptation in living color.

The urge to reach out and touch her taunted him, and he wondered—what would energy like hers feel like beneath his hands? Would she overwhelm him? Could he handle her or would he lose all control the second he made contact with her skin?

Turning the mug in his hand, he pushed away from the countertop. Good questions. No answers in sight. Not surprising. He'd never once touched a high-energy female. Never dreamed he'd get the chance, but longed to now. He wanted to strip her bare and stroke her skin. Yearned to immerse himself in the electrostatic current she threw off like pheromones and drown in her heat.

Breathing deep, he sifted through the scents in her tiny apartment, hunting for hers. Vanilla and sugar blended with the aroma of butter and melted chocolate, making it difficult to locate her fragrance in the mix. Taking a step toward her, he stopped beside the loveseat and...there. Right in front of his face, drifting on open air. Wallaig closed his eyes and inhaled again. Oh, man. So beautiful. She smelled delicious, tangy and tart...like lemon meringue pie, his favorite.

Lust chased a shiver down his spine.

He swallowed a groan. Goddess give him strength. Standing in the same room with her was torture, a special kind of masochism as hunger ate at his insides...and his dragon half seethed with need.

The beast wanted a taste.

Wallaig refused to allow it.

She was upset, her emotional grid reading like a chaotic ping-pong match. Back and forth. Advance and retreat. She couldn't decide how to feel about Elise's letters. Worry and anger dimmed her aura, tinging the fiery red-gold with bits of grey. Normal. To be expected considering she missed her best friend. But the more he studied her, the less he understood. What he was seeing didn't make sense. Something was wrong. Her emotion grid kept shifting, rising high and dipping low, warning him to look closer.

Using instinct as his guide, Wallaig mined her bio-energy. The complexity of her power burned across his senses. Hunger dug its claws deeper. He ignored the pain and searched harder, looking for—

His sonar pinged.

The energy pattern solidified and...aw, hell. Loneliness. Bone-deep despair. The fear she would forever be alone.

The realization grabbed hold of his heart and squeezed.

Sympathy bubbled up behind his breastbone.

Clenching his teeth, he drew another deep breath. Poor lass. Beautiful wee sprite. It wasn't right. The neglect she suffered cracked him wide open. A female as beautiful as Amantha shouldn't be alone. She deserved to be protected. To be desired and cherished. To be hugged and kissed and pampered until she purred with pleasure. A wise male would tell her how much he loved her...every damn day.

The thought was a dangerous one.

The kind he couldn't afford to entertain, but even as he tried to shut it down, he couldn't deny the truth. He wanted to be the male to hold and love her—to offer the comfort he knew she needed now more than ever. Sheer folly. Damned insane. He didn't know her. Had spent less than twenty minutes in her presence. Toss in the fact he couldn't stay and...shite. He was an idiot, a besotted slog with more testosterone than brains. Getting involved with Amantha wasn't a good idea. Not with Grizgunn on the hunt and his pack at war.

The attack on his home—the Scottish pack's mountain lair—made that all too clear.

The enemy lurked around every corner. Elise and Ivy had barely survived the first ambush, so...aye. Without a doubt. Introducing a new female into the pack qualified as a dumb idea. And yet, that didn't stop him from wanting to say "fuck safe" and embrace the unknown. Aye, it was sudden. A bit ridiculous too, given he didn't have her agreement, but as *no-can-do* morphed into *maybe*, he wanted to close the distance. Seek. Find. Claim. Two pieces of the puzzle were already in place—he'd found her. Now, all he needed to do was—

An image of him pulling her out of her chair and into his lap winged through his mind.

His thigh muscles twitched, begging him to move and take what he needed. Wallaig locked his knees, rooting his feet to the floor. He shook his head. Nay. Not going to happen. Dreaming about Amantha was all well and good. Taking her—claiming what didn't belong to him—was another thing entirely. Something he would do well to remember. And keep remembering until he unfolded his wings and flew for home.

"Hey, Wallaig?"

"Aye?"

"What does Elise mean by lair?" she asked. "She keeps mentioning it. Is it a house?"

"Kind of. It's where we live."

"Huh," she murmured, frowning at the page. "At least there's a library there. She says it's beautiful and has one of the best rare book collections in the world."

"All true, lass. Cyprus gave the collection to her as a mating gift."

"A what?" Her nose wrinkled as she threw him a perplexed look. "Do you mean wedding present?"

"Nay. 'Tis a mating gift in our culture."

"I don't understand."

"I know." Stepping around the end table, Wallaig sat down on the loveseat. Coils creaked, protesting his bulk as he leaned forward and set his forearms on his knees. "And I cannae explain."

"Why not?"

"Some things are meant to stay a secret, *kazlita*," he murmured, calling her sweetheart in Dragonese. A dumb ass move. He shouldn't be giving her a pet name. Endearments were reserved for mated females...for when a male staked his claim. Wallaig cringed inside. He was off the rails, acting the fool, saying things he shouldn't, wishing for a future that would never exist. "'Tis safer that way."

"For who?"

"You."

Her brow furrowed. "None of this makes sense. Something about the letters are odd."

"How so, lass?"

Amantha glanced down at the one she held, then back at him. "I don't know. I can't put my finger on what's wrong with them exactly. I mean, all the words are here...the sentences and paragraphs. It sounds right, and yet, I don't understand a thing. She seems happy. Says she loves him, but..."

Wallaig raised a brow, encouraging her to keep talking.

She flapped the letter in her hand. "I'm confused."

"About what?"

"It's weird. I know Elise, Wallaig. We've been best friends since sixth grade. We've never kept secrets from one another." Nibbling on her thumb nail. Amantha shook her head. "Something is missing in these pages, as though she couldn't bring herself to write the whole truth. And also..."

Pausing, she shuffled the papers, tucking one page behind another. "These are personal letters, more like journal entries. It's as though she wrote them for herself, not for me and...well, I'm not sure she intended for me to see them."

He huffed. Smart lass. Very astute. "She didn't, Amantha. Elise wanted to email you and explain. Her mate told her no, that it was too dangerous. He worries continued contact with Elise will place you in jeopardy."

"Why?"

"I cannae say."

"Then why are you here?" she asked, fisting the letters in her lap. Paper crinkled as she glared at him. "Why am I holding these?"

"Because I decided it was worth the risk. I thought you should know your friend is safe. And Elise will feel better now that you know."

Amantha blinked. A second later, her frustration shifted into appreciation. "Thank you."

"My pleasure."

"Will you get in trouble?" she asked, worry in her voice.

"Shite, I hope so," he said, her concern for him lighting a fire in his gut. "I haven't taken a chunk out of Cyprus in over a month."

She huffed, then shook her head. "Who's Cyprus?"

"He's not mentioned by name in the letters?" Wallaig frowned. Huh. Guess he'd missed that as he'd scanned Elise's private papers without permission.

"No."

"Cyprus is your friend's mate."

"Is that like a husband?"

"Aye. Exactly like one." Kind of, but not really. Dragonkind males mated for life, the bond so strong divorce didn't exist. The word *mate* meant something, was important and revered, an honor-bound tradition, unlike the use of *husband* in the human world. "They said their vows last week."

"Then why didn't you just say that?"

"Cultural differences, lass. We have our own way of saying things."

Staring at him as though he'd sprouted antlers, she pursed her lips. "You realize that's weird, right?"

"Mayhap, but it works."

"Wait a minute." Sitting forward in her chair, she treated him to a concerned look. "You're not in a cult, are you? 'Cause you know, that would explain a lot."

He snorted. Plucky lass. Charming as hell too. Wallaig couldn't contain a smile as he shook his head. "Not a cult. A family. A very close knit one."

"Oh," she whispered. Her aura flared. He tensed, struggling to maintain control as her bio-energy blasted him, then downgraded, dipping into loneliness. Again. For the fifth fucking time in as many minutes. "That sounds nice."

"It is." Reacting to the hurt in her voice, he shifted to the edge of his seat, wanting to touch her, knowing he shouldn't. She tried to smile. Tried to be brave. Tried to be happy for his good fortune. A sad attempt at best and...bloody hell. He disliked seeing her upset. His dragon snarled in outrage, then disconnected his brain from his mouth, forcing him to ask, "Would you like to meet them?"

Her eyes widened. Uncurling her legs, she sat upright in her chair. Her bare foot knocked into the coffee table, making the tea in her untouched mug slosh. "Really? You'd take me to see Elise?"

Wrestling his dragon back under control, he sucked in a breath. Jesus Christ. What in the hell had he just done? Nothing good. Something completely idiotic. Talk about sticking his paw in it. He couldn't take her home. Couldn't claim and keep her. Peril paved the way along that path.

He didn't give a damn about what his dragon wanted. The bastard could disagree all he liked. Wallaig refused to give in to impulse. Desiring Amantha wasn't enough. Craving her presented the kind of problems he couldn't allow. He needed to reverse course. Nip his growing attraction in the bud and backpedal as though his feet were on fire.

So...nothing for it. He must explain without hurting her.

How? The hell if he knew, but one thing remained clear. She couldn't come with him. He needed to make her understand, but as he opened his mouth, hope exploded in her aura, making her blaze with happiness. His chest tightened. The words he wanted to say got stuck in his throat. Bloody hell. He was in serious trouble. Was falling victim to the excitement on her face and the trust growing in her heart.

He needed to man-up—right now. Retract the invitation. Tell Amantha no. Walk out the door and never look back.

The idea left a bad taste in his mouth.

Wallaig pushed past the pain and shoved temptation aside.

Keeping her wasn't an option. He refused to set her down in the middle of a war. The second he did, he put a price on her head. With a growl, he reached for resolve. Time to step into the breech and tell Amantha the truth. She was better off forgetting about her friend. Better off, much safer, living in her own world than the violent reality of his. His enemies would show no mercy, which meant, like it or not, neither could he.

7

He was going to change his mind. Wallaig regretted extending her the invitation. Amantha could tell by the look on his face. Hardly conclusive. A pretty thin reason to believe he was about to ditch her. She swallowed past the lump forming in her throat. Reading another person's expressions wasn't her forte, but as disappointment hit her where it hurt, intuition backed up the conclusion.

He felt sorry for her.

Much like someone would when coming across a stray dog in the street.

The realization made her chest ache. His pity should've pissed her off. Should've stiffened her spine, made her shrug and say she didn't care. Too bad she'd never been good at lying to herself. Nothing good came from sticking her head in the sand, and as Wallaig laced his fingers between the spread of his knees and leaned toward her—no doubt about to break the news he planned to leave without her—Amantha didn't want to accept it.

Not like she had all those times growing up.

She'd learned a few things in the last couple of years. Now, she knew how to ask for what she needed.

And like it or not, the entire situation wore NEED like a label. She needed to see her best friend. Needed out of her tiny apartment. Needed to feel like a part of something...if only for a day. But most of all, and perhaps the worst, she didn't want Wallaig to leave her behind.

The admission startled her a little.

Amantha frowned. No way should she be this attached to a guy she'd just met. She'd spent a total of fifteen minutes in his company. Just enough time to scratch the surface—to know he possessed a good heart, a generous one given he'd risked his neck to bring her Elise's letters. Maybe that was her problem. Wallaig had been kind to her. Patient too, sitting with her, answering questions, helping her figure things out. But as she stared at him, something odd happened...her interest in him turned into full blown infatuation. Not smart. Nowhere near advisable, but somehow, completely unavoidable.

"Amantha," he murmured, his voice so deep vibrations erupted inside her, setting off an odd chain reaction.

Tingles slid up her spine, over the tops of her shoulders, then along the back of her head. A strange buzz started up between her temples.

He drew a breath, no doubt about to say more.

She held up her hand, asking him to wait as the hum expanded. Her vision blurred as the prickling sensation boiled over, breaking through mental boundaries, broadening her horizons in ways she didn't understand. A click echoed inside her head. A connection formed, shifting perception, feeding her information, making awareness bloom. Like an airborne virus, his intentions entered her veins. And all of a sudden, she knew what he was thinking.

Wallaig didn't want to deny her. He wanted to take her home.

But something held him back.

Clinging to the connection, she searched for the reason. The answer came through loud and clear. God, it was weird, but she'd tapped into him somehow. Now, she picked his thoughts right out of thin air. He worried about her safety and his ability to protect her on the flight home. Was unsure how his dragon brothers would react to him breaking protocol and pack rules. Amantha drew in a much-needed breath as his words tumbled through her head. *The flight home. Protocol and pack rules. Dragon brothers.* Odd expressions. Ones most people never used, so...her eyes narrowed...why was Wallaig?

Done waiting, Wallaig shifted on the loveseat. "Listen, *kazlita*, I know what I said, but—"

"Okay, here's the plan," she said, cutting him off. She refused to let him offer the lame ass excuse running around inside his brain. No way would she accept being blown off. Not this time. Not while her head buzzed and the connection grew, tightening its hold, making the thought of him leaving untenable. She'd spent a lifetime being abandoned—first by her father, then by her mother, and lastly, by the foster care system—but not tonight...and not by Wallaig. In a flap, she threw the letters onto the coffee table and scrambled out of her chair. "Half an hour, and we're out of here."

Surprised by her sudden movement, he leaned back in his seat. "Half an hour?"

"I have another batch of muffins to make. Blueberry Oatmeal." Screw the bran muffins. Her client's customers would have to make do with a few less calories today. "I'll mix'em up fast and pop'em in the oven.

Twenty minutes, that's all it'll take. After that, I'll put the last batch in boxes. Frank has a key. He'll pick everything up and—"

He growled. "Who the hell is Frank?"

"The delivery guy. He drops the orders off for me at each cafe. Oh, and after that I'll pack a bag."

"A bag?"

"Of course, I'll need a few things," she said, talking fast, hoping to confuse him into going along. "I'll pack one for Elise too. Just a few of her favorite things. She left all her stuff behind, you know?"

Frowning behind his sunglasses, he opened his mouth to answer.

The timer buzzed.

"Great!" Clapping her hands, she treated him to a sunny smile, then sped past him into the kitchen. "The apple spice muffins are done. Perfect timing."

Mouth hanging open, he turned to watch her go.

With quick hands, she snatched oven mitts off the counter and slid to a stop in front of the double ovens. Holding her breath, praying he didn't say what he was thinking, she cranked both doors open and pulled the tins from the oven. A gorgeous mix of apple and spice rolled into the room. Wallaig rumbled his approval, the sound more growl than word.

"Would you like one? They're really good." Turning, she set her bounty on the cooling racks, tossed her oven mitts aside, and picked up a fork. She wiggled a muffin free with the tines and without looking, tossed it in his direction. The treat sailed through the air. A second before he caught it, she murmured, "Careful, it's hot."

He plucked her gift out of mid-air. "You think feeding me will change anything?"

"Yes," she said without knowing why. Pure conjecture driven by female intuition. "It'll keep your mouth shut for a few more minutes."

He snorted. "And after that?"

"I'll give you a scone. Or a piece of lemon cake. Maybe the entire loaf." Yes, lemon. Seemed like the right answer. For some reason, she knew lemon infused treats were his favorite. Nice information to have, but as Wallaig turned the muffin over in his hand, she wondered whether distracting him with sweets would be enough. She hoped so, but just in case, sweetened the deal by grabbing the butter dish from beside the toaster and pulling a knife from the utensil drawer. Amantha set the entire mess down at the end of the kitchen island. "Better with butter, don't you think?"

His lips twitched. He shook his head, but didn't shoot her down. Footfalls thumping, he walked over and picked up the knife. "You're a terror, lass."

"Maybe," she said, grinning.

Slathering butter on his muffin, he smiled back.

A ripple of awareness shivered through her. The connection strengthened, funnelling into a current that made her body buzz and her attraction to him grow. Heaven help her, he was something. So well put together. Handsome without a trace of frat boy, he was all man, no polish. All ruthless vibe and chiseled cheekbones. His height didn't hurt his cause either, and God...the way he moved, long lean muscles in concert with a confident stride made her hormones sing and dance and...make all kinds of lude suggestions behind the curtain.

Wallaig would no doubt be good in bed.

He carried himself like a man who know how to please a woman. Guys with lots of experience usually did, and as she liberated the last muffin from the tin and set it on the cooling rack, Amantha imagined the possibilities. Hot, sweaty sex with Wallaig. Oh, baby. He wouldn't be polite. He would take what he wanted, be bossy and demanding while giving his partner more pleasure than she could handle.

The image set off a firestorm inside her mind. Her cheeks heated. She wiggled where she stood beside the island, her libido awake for the first time in months. God, she wanted that—wanted him wrapped around her and...*merde*. Not the best thought. She needed to shut her inner sex tap off right now. She had muffins to make and no time to screw around. Wallaig might turn his fine ass toward the door any second and never look back.

Drawing in a fortifying breath, she took stock of the ingredients in front of her. Flour, sugar, a bag of oatmeal. Baking powder, salt, a pallet of eggs. Wooden spoons at the ready and...huh. No bowl. She glanced over her shoulder and spotted the clean ones across the kitchen.

"Hey, Wallaig?" Dragging the flour closer, she picked up a measuring up. "Could you grab the big bowl on the top shelf for me?"

A heartbeat passed. No answer.

Hand hovering above the bag, Amantha looked his way and stilled. Something was wrong. He didn't look right. Nor had he heard her. Ignoring her, he stood unmoving, brows furrowed, attention locked on the large windows in her living room.

His gaze snapped toward the ceiling. "Shite."

She put the measuring cup down. "What is it?"

"Trouble." Tossing what remained of his muffin aside, he stepped around the end of the island and into her personal space. "Do you have a winter coat, Amantha?"

"Yeah."

"What about warm boots?"

She nodded. "I've got a toque and mittens too. Why?"

"Where are they?"

"Coat rack," she said, pointing at the front entrance. "What's going on?"

Wallaig didn't answer. He herded her out of the kitchen, half carrying her towards the door. As his boots touched down on the welcome mat, he glanced at the ceiling again. A muscle ticked in his jaw. "We need to go."

"What—right now?"

"Aye."

"But my muffins."

"Forget about the bloody muffins. Here...." Grabbing her coat off the hook, he wrapped it around her. "Arms in."

Shock made her slow.

His impatient growl sped her up.

She shoved her arms into the sleeves as he knelt and picked up her boots. A large hand gripped her calf. Heat bled through her pyjama bottoms, sending tingles up her leg. He tugged. Deciphering the unspoken message, Amantha lifted her foot. With more speed than grace, Wallaig pulled on her made-for-twenty-below-zero Sorel's—first one, then the other. He laced up each one, treating her like a two-year-old, then stood and zipped her ski jacket as well. A hat went on her head. Her mittens got tugged out of her pocket and slipped onto her hands.

Five point five seconds...that's all it took for him to bundle her into her winter gear. For what purpose? She had no earthly idea. And no wonder. Her brain wasn't working right. Critical thinking—the capacity to reason and react—failed her. No need to look for another explanation. Nothing else explained why she stood stock-still, acting like a puppet, allowing him to pull her strings while staring at him as though he'd lost his mind.

"Let's go, lass. We need to move before they land on the roof."

Land on the roof? She frowned. Seriously? What the hell was he talking about? She opened her mouth to ask. Wallaig didn't give her the chance to voice the question. Yanking the door open, he lifted her off her feet and, without a backward glance, carried her out of her apartment and into the hall.

8

A thump sounded overhead. The lights flickered as the whine of metal under sharp claws drifted down the corridor. Cursing under his breath, Wallaig stopped halfway down the hallway. Time to backtrack. Taking the stairs up to the roof was no longer an option. Neither was going back to Amantha's apartment. Nothing but death lay in that direction now.

He needed a new plan.

Preferably one that didn't involve getting cornered by a rogue pack inside the building.

Tightening his hold on Amantha, he unleashed his magic. Energy coated the walls, rushing in all directions, washing over the neighborhood. Pushing the boundaries, he cast his net wide. Like a brilliant patchwork comprised of light, a grid expanded inside his mind giving him a map of the area. His sonar pinged and...shite. The enemy couldn't be accused of being stupid. Eight strong, the bastards arrived in force. His eyes narrowed as individual energy signatures popped up on his mental screen—six warriors in full flight, two others had just landed on the roof, cutting off his preferred avenue of escape.

Wallaig growled.

Amantha quivered against him.

"Shh." Palming the back of her head, he tucked her head beneath his chin. Unable to help himself, he stroked her hair, sifting through the soft strands, wanting nothing more than to comfort her. "It's all right, *kazlita*."

"Please don't lie to me. I feel your tension. You're worried. Don't ask me how I know, but I do." Small hands fisted in his jacket, she pressed closer. "Something is really wrong, isn't it? Who's after you?"

"No one." Not really. He'd covered his tracks too well, left no trace when he flew into Edinburgh, which meant...the rogues weren't after him. Hell, the idiots didn't yet know he stood in the building, so...cross that possibility off the list. Eliminate it as a matter of course. Which left only one other conclusion to draw.

The bastards had gotten a hold of Elise's address.

He bared his teeth. Fucking Grizgunn. The male never quit. He'd been at it for weeks. Attack after attack on the Scottish pack, his mission clear—hurt Cyprus anyway he could. Now, it appeared the rogue leader was backtracking, searching for the female Cyprus had rescued and now claimed as his own. Not good news for Amantha. The rogue's plan put a bull's eye on her back. Grizgunn wouldn't hesitate. The male lacked honor and enjoyed hurting humans. He wouldn't care that the high-energy female living in apartment seventeen wasn't Elise.

He would take Amantha instead.

The idea of her being hurt made his blood run hot. His temper stirred. He wanted to kill the bastard for flying into her neighborhood. For daring to land on her roof. For threatening the female he couldn't bring himself to let go.

"Wallaig?"

"Donnae be afraid," he said, hating the scent of her fear. "I'll get us out safely, but you must be strong and follow my lead. I need you to trust me, lass. Do you think you can do that?"

"Yes," she said without hesitation.

"Good girl." Her quick answer squeezed his heart, making his respect for her grow. "Let's move."

She nodded.

Taking her hand, he pivoted and headed for the central staircase. Not his first choice. Neither was going out the front door. Exiting via the street—like a fucking human—never amounted to a good idea. He needed to shift and get airborne, the quicker the better. Not an easy prospect from the sidewalk. Height equaled leverage and speed. He needed both to out-fly the rogues already in dragon form. Precious seconds would be wasted leaping up from between cars and tall buildings. His wings wouldn't catch as much air, but...Wallaig clenched his teeth. Beggars couldn't be choosers. With the bastards already on the roof, his second option had just become his best one if he held any hope of protecting Amantha from the arseholes invading her home.

His boots banged down the first set of steps.

Amantha lost her footing. Her hand jerked in his a second before she careened into him from behind. Without breaking stride, he grabbed the back of her coat and swung her off her feet. She squeaked in alarm. He refused to stop. Feet doing double time, he swung her up and around, throwing her onto his back. She landed with a muffled "ooh", but caught on fast, wrapping her arms and legs around him, riding piggyback style as he ran down the stairs.

He rounded the last landing.

The lobby came into view.

Headlights flashed against double glass doors as a car drove past the building.

Heart hammering, he slid to a stop beside the entrance. His back to the wall, Amantha still hanging on tight, he glanced outside. Nothing moved on the street. No humans out for a midnight stroll. No taxis waiting curbside. No dragons sitting on street corners. A clear path to the end of the avenue.

"All right." Reaching around, he cupped her cheek. She turned into his touch, receiving comfort, soothing him in return, then she pressed her mouth against his palm. A shiver of awareness rumbled through him. An odd prickle ghosted across the top of his shoulders. Suppressing a shiver, he gave her a gentle squeeze. "Hold on tight, lass. Donnae let go...no matter what happens."

"Got it."

Unable to help himself, he smoothed his thumb over her bottom lip. "Kiss me before we go."

A stupid request given the circumstances. Wallaig almost took it back, but...God. With her pressed against him, he couldn't resist her allure. He needed a taste. Just a wee one before he risked both of their lives and flew into danger.

"Please," he murmured, feeling foolish as the plea rose in the silence.

Her breath hitched, and he waited, hope beating as loudly as his heart.

Shifting her grip, Amantha held onto him with one hand, then lifted her chin and leaned in. Her mouth met his, the brush of her lips soft as butterfly wings. He groaned. She grew braver and pressed closer, demanding entrance. He opened for her, kissing her back, tangling his tongue with hers, giving her what she wanted, getting what he needed.

Bliss spun into the desire.

His hunger for her, banked but still burning, surged to the forefront. His dragon half rose, asking for more. Unable to resist, he took the kiss deeper. She hummed, tightening her hold on him as he gripped her wrist with one hand and cupped her throat with the other. Her bio-energy blazed into a torrent of current. His fingertips tingled. The Meridian crackled, plugging him into the powerful stream, allowing him his first real taste.

Greedy for her, he drank deep, drawing the nourishment he required to stay healthy and strong from her into his own veins. His beast hummed in approval. Amantha moaned and, with a wiggle, tried to get closer.

Wallaig didn't argue. No need to dissuade her. He kissed her back instead. Gave her all she asked, reveling in her response, thankful for what she so generously provided. And as she revived him, feeding him from the source, flooding him with pleasure, he knew he would never let her go. She belonged to him and, in that moment, he became hers. His dragon had decided. Energy-fuse was already taking hold. He sensed the bond growing, felt the connection, recognized his mate the second his skin touched hers.

No need to ask questions or deny the truth.

Nipping her bottom lip, he lifted his mouth from hers. "Hmm...you taste good, lass."

"So do you." Following his retreat, she kissed him softly.

He returned the caress. "Time to go."

"Okay, but we'll continue this later."

Goddess willing. He wanted her more than anyone

else in a long time. Needed her in ways he didn't yet understand, but instinct told him existed all the same.

Turning his attention back to the street, he shook his head. A mate. *His mate.* A female to call his own. The idea shocked him. He'd never considered he might find her—that she might want him in return. But as Amantha shifted on his back, hugging him tighter, and he got ready to move, his priorities reshuffled. She was here. He would claim her. But first, he had a gauntlet of enemy dragons to run...without much needed backup from his brothers-in-arms.

9

———

Crouched next to the front door, Wallaig slid Amantha off his back and conjured a cloaking spell. Magic snapped like a whip. Heat billowed up, blowing across the lobby as he and Amantha disappeared from view. A necessary illusion, one he knew wouldn't last long when he exited the building.

Leaning to one side, he glanced out the glass doors, then shook his head. Outnumbered and surrounded...not the greatest odds with a female to protect. Not that it mattered. All he needed was thirty seconds of cover. Enough time to get the lay of the land. Count the number of parked cars. Gauge the width of the intersections bookending the block. Find the best place to shift into dragon form and get airborne.

Simple enough plan. Huge consequences if he failed.

Every second counted.

The instant he transformed, the enemy would pinpoint him and mobilize. Launch a full-scale attack. Attempt to kill him before he gained the necessary altitude to defend himself. So aye, reaching open skies needed to happen in a hurry.

Dragging his gaze from the view of the street, he turned to look at Amantha. Aura ablaze, her features defined by bright light, her gaze met his. He held out his hand. Without hesitation, she slid her much smaller one into his.

"It's going to get bad, isn't it?"

"We'll be fine," he said, bending the truth, not wanting to frighten her. "But..."

"What?"

"You're going to see things you never have before." With a gentle tug, he drew her alongside him. She nestled in, holding his hand, pressing her cheek against his upper arm, trusting him to keep her safe. Dipping his head, he kissed her temple. Warm skin beneath his lips. Her scent all around him. His female in all her glory—the best off all reasons to protect, fight and annihilate. "Whatever happens...no matter how strange it seems to you...stay calm, lass."

"I'll try."

"'Tis all I can ask."

Gathering magical threads, Wallaig tightened the invisibility spell and nudged the door open. He stayed low, shielding Amantha as he slipped over the threshold and broke cover. Rain-soaked concrete met the soles of his boots. Puddles splashed underfoot. Well-oiled hinges creaked behind him. Wallaig didn't bother to look back. The soft sound wasn't a concern. None of the rogues would bother to investigate. Not for something so minor—a regular noise in a human neighborhood. What concerned him was the layout. Small cars parked along narrow avenues. Nothing tall enough to use as a launch pad. Crappy news given the terrain and bad odds.

Deep in the shadows, he crept along the building foundation. The wind shifted, bringing the scent of multiple dragons north of his position. He veered left, ran between parked cars and crossed the street. Amanda scurried along behind him, her fingers clutching him tight. Reaching an intersection, he gave her a reassuring squeeze and back pressed against a building, peered around the corner. Energy shifted and rolled, allowing him to see in the dark and...ah. Right there. Two bogies at one o'clock. Perched on the rooftop at the end of the block, the rogues sat on opposite ends of the building, attention locked on intersecting alleys below.

Wallaig glanced in the other direction.

His gaze landed on a moving truck parked curbside. Tall, white box. Sturdy construction. Less than thirty yards away. A quick calculation and...aye, the truck would do. Provide enough height he needed to get airborne...but only if he reached it in time.

He looked over his shoulder and checked on the rogues. Neither had moved. Good. The longer the pair remained oblivious, the better for him. Swiveling in his crouch, he drew Amantha from behind him. She settled between the spread of his thighs and pressed close, using him for balance. Wallaig wrapped his arms around her and scanned the area over the top of her head. He needed to be certain, know exactly where he was going the moment he moved. With so many rogues in the area, precise execution of the plan mattered.

He swept the street again, just to be sure.

A small car parked behind the target vehicle. No humans walking down the street. Pretty good set up, the best he would get tonight. Eyes locked on the truck, he loosened Amantha's grip on his jacket. She drew a shaky breath but complied, letting him go, allowing him to grip both of her wrists.

"Hold on, Amantha."

He didn't give her any other warning. Wallaig stood instead and, jerking her forward, threw her over his shoulder. Head down, arse up in the air, she hissed in surprise. Her legs kicked. He locked her down with an arm over her thighs and, legs pumping, sprinted toward the truck. His boots hammered the sidewalk. Sound detonated, echoing off concrete and metal, rolling down the block, giving away his position.

The cry of alarm went up.

Dragons took flight. The sound of flapping wings joined the thump of his footfalls.

Adrenaline burned through his veins. Heart hammering, muscles coiled, Wallaig ran faster. Almost there. Less than ten feet away. He took three more strides and, with a snarl, leapt from the sidewalk and—

Bang!

He landed on top of the car.

Steel dented beneath his feet. He didn't stop. Baring his teeth, he launched himself onto the top of the truck. His boots slid across the slick surface. Momentum hurled him toward the edge of the box. Not bothering to slow down, Wallaig transformed. Magic exploded in the air around him. Hands and feet turning into huge paws, his body lengthened under blood red scales. His spiked tail whiplashed. Amantha squeaked in alarm. Careful not to clip her with his claws, he cradled her in his palm and unfurled his wings. Needing more height, he flipped sideways in mid-air. His talons caught on a building façade. Chunks of stone crumbled, tumbling toward the sidewalk as he launched himself into the sky.

Wind-rush rattled his scales.

Building tops came into view.

A glint of green flashed in his periphery.

Baring his fangs, Wallaig roared in challenge. With a quick twist, he spun toward the threat. The rogue's eyes widened, and Wallaig struck, lashing out with his tail. Razor-sharp spikes slammed into the male. The rogue's head whiplashed. Dragon teeth flew as blood arched through the air. Shielding Amantha, he hammered the rogue again. And again. One more time, and...green scales cracked wide open. The enemy screamed in agony.

Showing no mercy, Wallaig slashed through the rogue's wing. He plummeted out of the sky, falling fast as his buddy flew to the rescue.

Wings spread wide, he banked hard. The blue dragon lashed out. Sharp claws raked his scales. Pain burst across his rib cage. Gritting his teeth, he twisted into a backflip. The rogue tried to counter, but...too late. In prime position, Wallaig boxed him in and unleashed a roundhouse. His elbow slammed into the side of the male's skull. The crack resonated as he somersaulted up and over. Halfway through the rotation, he grabbed the rogue by a horn. He yanked, dragging the pup sideways in mid-air. As the idiot yelped, he whirled into a mind-splitting spin.

One. Two. On three, he let go.

Unable to control the velocity, the male slammed snout-first into a concrete wall. Bone snapped. The crack ricocheted as more blood splashed up and out.

Ignoring his artwork splattered across building facades, Wallaig scanned the sky.

Four more dragons took flight.

Wallaig cursed. Time to retreat. He couldn't get caught out in the open. Not again. Fighting rogues one and two had been necessary. Something he hadn't been able to avoid. But no longer. He was airborne, in full flight with a wide-open sky behind him. No need to push his luck.

Whipping around, he ignored the roar of enemy dragons and rocketed it in the opposite direction. He needed to kill time until daybreak. A place to hide and settle Amantha would be best. Somewhere the rogues wouldn't think to look. Daylight—and deadly UV rays —would do what he couldn't right now: turn the bastards around. So...new strategy. Keep ahead of Grizgunn, lose the bastards in the city, find somewhere to hold up until the sun chased the enemy pack inside for the day.

Speed supersonic, Wallaig shot across the night sky. Bright light burned across his senses as he searched for a safe place to set down. Where? Where could he go? What area held the most promise? He frowned. The warehouse district might work. Located next to the Port of Edinburgh, the area was more labyrinth than business hub. The fact that section of the city was surrounded by water and...

His eyes narrowed. Aye. It just might work.

The water would muffle his energy signal. A definite plus given the horde now hunting him. The fact most dragons feared water wouldn't hurt either. The rogue pack wouldn't search hard near the shoreline. The bastards would assume what all of Dragonkind knew—no dragon worth his salt would use water as a means of escape. Under normal circumstances, Wallaig would've agreed, but the port presented a real advantage. One he refused to ignore...no matter how much he disliked the ocean.

Wallaig grimaced. Goddess give him strength. Was he really thinking about it? He wasn't a strong swimmer. Cringed at the very idea of being under water but with Amantha curled into the fetal position, he'd brave anything. Wet scales included to ensure she stayed hale and whole.

Flying low, playing hide and seek with the rogues on his tail, Wallaig skimmed rooftops and picked his way toward the harbour. Lit up like Christmas, bright lights glowed above concrete piers and squat buildings. Tall cranes towered over ocean freighters piled high with steel containers. Exhaust spilled into the air, making his nose twitch as he spotted humans on the ground.

He spread his wings. His speed slowed to a glide. A dangerous move, one that allowed the rogues to gain ground. His sonar pinged as the enemy closed within a mile of him. Wallaig clenched his teeth. He couldn't stay here. Too many human wearing hardhats milling around. He must move on before Grizgunn caught up and he ended up cornered again.

Hugging Amantha tighter, he assessed his options. Not the new warehouses next to the pier. Forget about the ship in dry dock. The fishing boats moored to the docks further down might work, but...nay. None of the locations would work as places to hide. He needed to move away from the shoreline, otherwise Grizgunn would ferret him out before the sun rose and—

A rumble broke through the clang of heavy cranes moving containers.

Wallaig's attention snapped toward the outer harbour.

Lines trailing in the water, a tugboat pulled away from a dock.

As he watched, the captain manoeuvred through water traffic and, nose breaking through waves, chugged toward a large freighter exiting the port.

His sonar pinged again. Information streamed into his head, giving him the rogue pack's location. Half a mile away now. Goddamn it. He was out of time. The bastards were almost on top of him.

Wallaig hesitated a second, then folded his wings and drove toward the water. He entered without making a splash and plunged deep. Cold water closed around him. He flinched, but held the line, more concerned about Amantha than himself. She jerked against him. He heard her yell underwater. Cupping both paws around her, he created an air pocket, feeding her oxygen as he struggled swim.

He needed to reach the tugboat motoring above him. A rope attached to the gunnel lay in the water, streaming alongside the boat. A literal lifeline, the only means of escape as he sensed the enemy fly over the harbor.

Holding his breath, he swished his tail like an alligator and swam toward the boat. A moment before he broke the surface, he shifted to human form. Amantha sputtered. Cradling her in one arm, he reached for the line with the other. His fingers caught hold. Rope burned across his palm. Wallaig tightened his grip, keeping his female's head above the surf as the tugboat began to tow him alongside it.

He coughed up water. "Fucking hell."

"No kidding." Clinging to him, Amantha wheezed against his throat. "What the hell was that?"

She sounded pissed off. Wallaig didn't blame her. He hadn't shown her a very good time tonight. "Sorry."

Wet eyelashes blinking furiously, she scowled. "You...you...you..."

"Lass, if you'll just—"

"You're a maniac!" she yelled, following the insult up with a string of French words he didn't understand.

Wallaig jerked his head back as she pointed her finger at him. Wow. The lass owned a temper...and an impressive vocabulary. He didn't understand much French, but...he blinked. Had she just called him a bug-eyed toad? Amusement boiled over, threatening to make an appearance on his face. Not smart given her outburst, but...Christ. He couldn't help himself. She was adorable. A true treat to watch as her bio-energy flared, and she yelled some more, going head mistress on his arse. A hotter than hell head mistress with narrowed eyes and pink cheeks, shooting sparks and fire.

She called him another name.

His lips twitched.

"Don't laugh, Wallaig. Don't you dare." Hitching herself higher on his chest, she went nose to nose with him. "You should have warned me."

"I did. I warned you it might get—"

"Not well enough," she snapped, looking like a thundercloud. "You should have told me."

"About dragons?"

Hat askew, she slapped wet hair out of her eyes with a soggy mitten. "Yes!"

"How the hell was I supposed to do that?" he asked, his tone more defensive than he liked. "Would you have believed me?"

The question stopped her mid-tirade. She pursed her lips. "No, probably not. You may have a point."

"Thank God. About time I got one on my side of the board." Wrapping the rope around his wrist, he turned onto his back, putting them breast to chest. Seaweed streamed along his arm, then swirled past Amantha. She shivered. With a murmur, Wallaig called on his magic. Heat bubbled up, warming the water, ensuring she didn't catch a chill. "Give me a break, would you, Amantha? It's not as though I've done this before."

"What—rescue a girl?" she asked, aura settling into normal levels as her temper faded. Kicking out with her legs, she paddled her feet, re-establishing her hold on his jacket. "I should probably thank you for that."

"You're welcome, *kazlita*. I know I threw you into the thick of it, but I..." The tugboat throttled down. He paused, listening to the engines whine, struggling to find the right words. "I couldn't leave you behind."

Her brow furrowed. "But you thought about it."

"For a split second," he murmured. "And only before the rogues showed up."

"Those other dragons?"

"Aye."

Confusion bloomed in her eyes. "How is any of this possible? It's just not...I mean...how can you be... God, Wallaig. You're a dragon."

Her whisper lashed at his heart. Of course, she was shocked. Stood to reason. She should be after learning Dragonkind existed in her tidy little world. "I'm no different than you, Amantha."

She treated him to a please-pull-your-head-out-of-your-arse look. "You can't be serious. Not after what I just witnessed."

His mouth curved. "All right, maybe a little different."

Amantha huffed.

"I am Dragonkind, lass," he said, keeping it simple. No need to go into detail yet. He didn't want her running scared. Her questions would come...eventually. Until then, he planned to provide the basics, and not a nanobite more. "We're a different species—half human, half dragon. No less, naught more."

"But no one knows you exist."

"We like it that way."

"I can imagine. Less dragon slayers to worry about."

"Exactly," he said, plucking a piece of seaweed from her hair.

The tugboat bumped into something. Wallaig swayed into the hull. As his shoulder rubbed against steel, rubber squeaked along the side of the ocean freighter. Throttle clicking, the captain put his boat in neutral. Big engines rumbled, kicking up water at the stern. A firm hold on the rope, he pulled his female closer and glanced up at the gunnel above his head. "Ready to get out of the water?"

"God, yes, but..." Frowning, she gripped his shoulders, then twisted to look behind her. "Are the bad guys gone?"

Fine-tuning his sonar, Wallaig scanned the sky over warehouses and granite piers. No pings on his mental radar. No bursts of light. Not an enemy energy signal in sight over the harbour. "For now."

Concern dimmed her aura. "But not for good?"

"We'll worry about that later. Let's get you warm and dry first, lass."

"Okay," she said, sounding unsure.

The need to comfort her jabbed at him. Taking a chance, he dipped his head. His lips brushed the corner of hers. She murmured against his mouth. He kissed her again, enjoying her taste, keeping it light... and Amantha let him. Amazing news considering nothing was set in stone. Energy-fuse might be a wondrous thing, but it didn't mean she wouldn't run scared and reject him out of hand.

A bad outcome. A distinct possibility the second her feet touched down on solid ground.

Not everyone could handle the truth. Or turn away from the world they knew to begin again in a new one. But as he climbed the rope with Amantha on his back, her welcoming response gave him hope. Maybe—if he got really, *really* lucky—she would be brave, embrace the unknown and claim him for her own.

10

Nerves stretched so thin her muscles felt like wet noodles, Amantha allowed Wallaig to lift her over the railing and onto the deck of the ocean freighter. How he managed to the scale the smooth steel hull, she didn't know. Didn't care to either. She'd refused to look, squeezing her eyes closed, pressing her face against the nape of his neck, trying to pretend she wasn't clinging to a guy climbing the side of a ship.

An idiotic thing to do. She never stuck her head in the sand. Facing things was more her style, but...not tonight. No matter how independent she strived to be, she ended up relying on Wallaig. Damned embarrassing. A bit of a setback on the feminist front but after all the crazy dragon stuff, she couldn't handle any more. No hiccups. Zero bumps. Just a whole lot of smooth sailing on the way to wherever he was taking her.

She hoped it was somewhere warm. Being half frozen wasn't any fun.

Drawing a shaky breath, Amantha pried her hands from the lapels of his coat. Her fingers burned with the cold, making her joints ache and her skin hurt. A shiver rattled her bones. Wallaig cursed and, pulling her closer, yanked off her mittens. Tossing the soggy pair over his shoulder, he cupped her hands. Heat streamed from him into her, making her moan in gratitude.

Another tremor racked her. "God, you're so warm."

"The upside of being a fire dragon." Dipping his head, he blew hot air on her fingers.

"Fantastic perk."

"No question," he murmured, his tone as warm as his body. "Especially after being dunked in a harbor."

"In the middle of winter." A snowflake drifted past her nose. Water dripped off the hem of her coat, leaving puddles on the deck. Her teeth started to chatter. "We're not doing that again, are we?"

"Nah, we're going to steal a bed instead."

The news gave her hope. "Where?"

He tipped his head toward the stern of the freighter. "Inside. Ships like this always have empty cabins...a suite for corporate VIPs. How be we find it?"

She nodded, liking the plan.

Shifting focus, he transferred both of her hands into one of his, sharing his heat as he turned toward the afterhouse and headed toward the back of the ship. Large steel hatches covered the cargo holds, tall booms rising between each one. She didn't know a lot about boats, but the one she stood on seemed like a good one, capable of carrying vast amounts of cargo to ports all over the world. An efficient machine. Beautiful in its own way, and...Amantha glanced around at the deck. Smooth steal, no dings or dents, not a rusty spot in sight. Even the smokestack boasted a coat of shiny red paint.

Her gaze jumped to the bridge on the top floor of

the afterhouse. Men stood behind wide windows, busy navigating the ship out of the port and—

Amantha jolted. "Can they see us?"

"Nay, lass, not while we're cloaked. Donnae worry."

She blinked. "We're cloaked?"

"Aye. Completely invisible to human eyes."

"Another of those dragon perks."

"A necessary one," he said, stepping around a large spool bolted to the deck. "Can you imagine what would happen if humans saw a pack of dragons flying around late at night."

"Keys to nuclear launch codes would get dusted off."

He snorted.

Her mouth curved, reacting to his amusement. "Why only late at night?"

"Dragonkind doesn't tolerate sunlight."

"At all?"

His expression tightened. Wallaig shook his head. "UV rays burn our scales and damage our eyes. If one of my kind stays out too long, the sun will reduce him to ash."

The quiet fury in his tone put her on high alert. Her hands flexed around his much larger one. The strange connection she sensed growing between them flickered, then opened like a faucet inside her head. Pain and anger poured through the link, making her stomach dip and her chest go tight. And just like that, she could feel him—all the anguish Wallaig fought to hide and...oh, God. Something bad had happened to him. Something to do with the sun.

Instinct guiding her, she rubbed her cheek against his arm. "What happened, Wallaig? Did you stay out too long and get burned?"

He stopped mid-stride. His chin dipped a moment before his brows furrowed behind his wraparounds. One second ticked into more as she stood unmoving, wanting to give him space, needing him to speak. She didn't push him for an answer. Amantha waited instead, heart thumping, worry for him rising, so desperate to ease his pain she ached on the inside. A strange reaction, one she didn't understand. Couldn't begin to explain either. What she felt for him—his odd hold on her—bordered on insanity. He was half dragon, a man who shifted forms at will, a completely different species. And yet, as she held her breath, praying he would open up and tell her what was wrong, she realized he didn't scare her.

Wallaig would never hurt her.

He'd proven it over and over tonight.

"If you don't want to tell me," she said. "I'll understand. It's just—"

"One of my brothers-in-arms betrayed our pack and I got ambushed. I was injured in the fight and woke up in a field north of Aberdeen." A muscle twitched along his jaw as he took off his sunglasses and turned to face her. "I didn't make it home in time."

Raising his lashes, he met her gaze for the first time.

Amantha's breath hitched. Merde de dieu. He was blind, his irises so badly scarred each one flashed white in the dim light. Empathy hit her like a hurricane, ripping her out by the roots. Unmoored, unable to help herself, she reached up to touch his face. Her fingertips brushed over his cheekbones just below his eyes. Tense beneath her hands, he allowed the caress. Needing to ease his despair, she rose onto her tiptoes and pressed her lips to his eyelid—first one, then the other, trying to kiss away the pain.

"I'm so sorry," she whispered against his skin. "It isn't fair."

"Fairness doesn't count for much in my world," he murmured, holding still as she kissed him again. "Donnae feel sorry for me, lass. I'm not completely blind. I see in my own way."

She opened her mouth to ask him how.

"Come, *kazlita*." With a gentle tug, Wallaig got her moving, then walked toward the stairs at the base of the afterhouse. "Dawn will arrive any minute. We need to get inside."

Towing her behind him, he took the steps two at a time. Feet banging on steel treads, Amantha kept pace, staying right behind him. But as Wallaig reached the landing, pulled the heavy door open and guided her inside, she faltered. She had so many questions. And not nearly enough answers. Which meant time to put the screws to Wallaig and find out exactly what being with him entailed...before she got in so deep she couldn't get out.

11

Navigating a narrow corridor, Wallaig glanced at the plaque on each door until he came to one that read CAPTAIN in big bold letters. The cabin he searched for wouldn't be far now. Human VIPs expected the best, liked to be pampered, so...aye. The corporate suite aboard the ship must be close. Maybe around the bend, in the next corridor. Stood to reason. No way would a spoiled executive consent to being placed on a lower level next to the crew.

A harsh conclusion to draw maybe, but...

He shrugged. He didn't care. Human males were a mystery he held no interest in solving. The female trailing him, however, was a whole other matter. He wanted to know

Amantha in every way—as a friend and lover, as a male in thrall to his mate. The realization made him huff in amusement. Hell, cross *enthralled* off the list. He was already enchanted, so attuned to her he sensed her thoughts, felt her breath and knew without looking she still shivered from the cold.

Biting down on a curse, Wallaig picked up the pace. He needed to get her out of her clothes. Wet and cold didn't go well together. She was already catching a chill and...goddamn it. He should've found a better way to evade the enemy. What that escape route would've been, he didn't know. Diving into the harbor had been both the best and most expedient way of losing the bastards, but he hated that his female suffered. Lacing her chilled fingers through his, he turned down another hallway. She lost her footing and bumped into his back. His chest went tight as the level of her exhaustion registered. His fault...all his fault, her fatigue one hundred percent his doing. If only he had—

"How much further, Wallaig?" Amantha asked, teeth chattering.

Up ahead, he spied the label next to a door: EXECUTIVE SUITE. He exhaled in relief. Thank God. About time he had some good news to give her. "Just there, *kazlita*. We'll be inside in a moment."

With a pronounced shiver, she nodded.

Wrapping his arms around her, he pulled her to his chest, sharing his heat as he stopped in front of the door. He disengaged the lock with a thought. Metal scraped against metal. The tumblers turned. With a flick of the handle, he shoved the door open, picked up Amantha, and cradling her in his arms, strode inside. A quick glance gave him the layout. Sitting area with a couch and chairs to his left fronted by large windows. He murmured, issuing a command. The curtains closed, moving around steel tracks, blocking out the glow of sunlight on the horizon, plunging the suite into darkness. Ignoring the queen size bed up against one wall, he moved toward what he assumed to be the ensuite bath.

He crossed the threshold. Large shower with fancy green and white tile. Separate tub on the opposite side of the room. Double sinks in a marble countertop. Wallaig grunted. Nice set-up, and the perfect place to drive the chill from Amantha's bones.

Setting her down, he unzipped her coat and stripped it off her. He threw the wet mess into the corner and crouched at her feet. As he unlaced her boots, he turned on the shower with his mind. Water rushed from the shower head, splattering across ceramic tile.

Amantha flinched. "Did you do that?"

"Aye," he said, tossing her Sorels alongside her jacket.

"How?"

"Magic, lass. Another of those perks you like so much."

"P-pretty c-cool," she said, sounding half frozen.

"It has its moments."

"I'll bet," she said with a huff, trying to laugh.

She didn't quite make it. Amantha was too cold to pull off levity but shite, he admired her spirit. His mouth curved. Goddess, she was beautiful, so smart and strong. Everything he hadn't known he needed and couldn't believe he'd found. Such a strange turn of events. A bundle of letters had brought him to her door, and as he waited for the water to warm, the near miss made him frown. If not for his insubordination —disobeying a direct order from his commander—he wouldn't be here. Would never have met her. Wouldn't be touching her now, never mind seeing to her needs.

The realization tightened his chest.

He might not know Amantha well yet, but already he longed for a future with her. Wanted to take her to bed each morning and wake in her arms every afternoon. Absolute acceptance. Real connection. A female to share his life, a mate whom he could love and be loved by in return.

Yesterday, it had been a pipedream. Nothing but smoke and mirrors, the stuff of myths. But as he knelt at her feet, his dream took shape and form, placing her at the center of it.

"Amantha," he murmured, his tone so reverent his heart panged and longing took hold. Skimming his hands up her legs, he gripped her hips and hooked his fingers beneath the waistband of her pyjamas. "Fair warning, lass...I'm going to strip you down now."

"What?"

"You need to get out of your wet pyjamas."

"But I don't have anything on underneath," she said with a squeak.

"Perfect." Amused by her modesty, he dragged the pants down her legs. Soft skin grazed his palms as the flannel bottoms fell, leaving her bare from the waist down.

"Wallaig!"

Entranced by the sight and feel of her, he growled. Unable to stop himself, he nipped the top of her knee, then dragged his mouth along the length of her thigh. She made a soft sound of surprise. He jumped to her belly, pressing his lips against her skin.

Her breath hitched. A quiver shook her, this one not driven by the cold. She whispered his name. Her hand touched his head, clever fingers delving into his hair as she welcomed his attention.

"Take your t-shirt off, lass. The water's ready." Ghosting left, he licked over her hipbone.

She gasped, the sound full of delight.

Wallaig stood and, grabbing the cotton hem of her tee, dragged it over her head.

As she sucked in a breath, he shucked his clothes,

tossed them in his mental vault and...oh, aye. Skin on skin. Breast to chest. His erection pressed to the softness of her belly. Oh, so good. The absolute best way to start the day. Wallaig groaned, fighting for control as he cupped her bottom and moved toward the shower. The door opened upon command. He crossed the threshold, enclosing Amantha in the stall with him. The glass slider closed. Warm steam billowed up, surrounding him, warming his mate. Taking her with him, he stepped beneath the steady stream of hot water.

She sighed in relief.

The gorgeous sound wound him tighter.

Brushing wet hair away from her face, he kissed her again. His female met and matched him, lifting her chin, opening her mouth, asking him for more. He should say no. A smart male would keep it light, give her time to get to know him, instead of giving into desire. But as Amantha cupped the back of his head and deepened the kiss, Wallaig knew he was lost.

He needed her.

She wanted him.

Fuck too fast, too soon. He would take what she offered, give her explosive pleasure in return, and hope like hell she didn't regret it when she woke in his arms.

12

He tasted so good, like an aphrodisiac dipped in chocolate. Sweet. Addictive. Better than anything she'd ever taken out of the oven. A helluva lot hotter too.

Steam rising around her, she stood on tiptoe and tried to get closer, wanting to absorb Wallaig into her skin. The shower head sputtered. Warm water washed over her and splashed on to him as she pressed her breasts to his chest. He growled in approval and big hands roaming, caressed the sensitive crease where the top of her thigh met her bottom. Pleasure coursed through her and...mercy, he was hot. All hard muscles and busy hands.

He took her mouth like he owned her, sharing his taste, delighting her with his possession. With a hum, Amantha kissed him back and sent her own hands wandering. She skimmed over his shoulders, then stroked along his biceps. So strong. So gorgeous with his messy auburn hair and the stubble on his angular face. She loved the feel of it—the brush of his beard against her lips as he shifted against her.

Gentling the kiss, he retreated. Not a lot. Hardly any distance at all, just enough to cup her breast. His hand engulfed her. Heat hit her like a sledgehammer, arching her spine, pushing her into his palm, forcing a plea from her throat.

Wallaig didn't deny her. He explored her instead, adjusting the pressure, making delight danced along her spine. Gasping, she tried to catch her breath. He refused to let her, tangling their tongues, taking control until she surrendered. His murmured "good lass" was her reward. She shuddered in his arms. Closer… she needed him closer. Wanted him so deep inside her, she forgot where he ended and she began and—

He flicked her nipple, rolling the sensitive nub between her fingers.

Amantha cried out and arched her back, wanting more, needing less and…God, she didn't know anymore. His scent caused her head to spin. His taste made her crave him more and…

What the hell was happening to her? She'd gone from cold to hot in an instant. Was so needy impatience grabbed the wheel, drove her straight into desire, then ran over common sense. She heard the crash. Felt the jolt. Heard mental barriers buckle as her mind gave way to her long-neglected libido.

Not the greatest plan in the history of womankind.

Sleeping with a man on a first date wasn't the best idea. Caution always served a girl well. But as Wallaig caressed her, learning her body, sensitizing her skin, Amantha refused to play it safe. Not today. She yearned to be wild, if only for a little while. For once, she didn't care what happened in the aftermath. Tomorrow would take care of itself. Right now, she needed Wallaig to take care of her. Longed for what his touch promised—the fast burn of frenzied bliss.

Fisting her hands in his hair, she hopped up and wrapped her legs around his waist. The quick shift took him by surprise. He cursed. She wiggled, adjusting their fit, pressing her core against his erection and—

Holy Moses. "Do that again."

"Amantha, hold on a—"

Buried in bliss, she rolled her hips. Slick with need, she slid against him, bucking with every tiny jolt of pleasure. God, she was close. So close. He'd hardly touched her, and she was almost there, right on the edge, about to go over. Locking her ankles at his back, she upped the pace, reaching for the pinnacle.

With a snarl, Wallaig grabbed her hips. Calloused fingers on her bottom, he broke her rhythm. "Bloody hell, Amantha. Slow down."

"No," she gasped, flexing her thighs, fighting his control.

"You're rushing it, lass."

"I know, but I just..." She moaned, arching in pleasure as he turned and pressed her back to the shower wall. "I can't help it. I'm so close. I need more."

Sharp teeth nipped her pulse point. "You get what I give you."

"Then give me everything, Wallaig." Breathing hard, she squirmed, desperate for relief. "Pleeease."

"Fuck. I thought to be gentle with you the first time."

"Next time," she whispered, her orgasm glimmering just out of reach. "Next time."

"Deal, but first..." Grabbing her foot, he unlocked her ankles from the base of his spine. "You're going to give me a taste."

Delivered on a growl, his words sounded ominous. His actions backed up the treat as he flattened his palm on her breastbone, immobilizing her against the wall, then slid down her body. He paid homage along the way—nipping the tip of her breast, planting kisses on her belly, stroking over the curve of her bottom—before kneeling at her feet. Hooking her legs over his shoulders, he spread her thighs wide, opening her to his touch.

Hot breath rushed over her core.

His tongue lashed her, licking into her folds. Back pressed to the wall, imprisoned by the position, Amantha keened as ecstasy pulsed through her. She grew slicker. Wallaig groaned and delved deeper, leaving no part of her untouched. No part of her untasted. Over and over. Again and again. He took what he wanted, stopping to suck on her clitoris, pushing her so high she begged for the pleasure.

He brought his fingers into play. One thrust deep. A second joined the first, stroking against a sensitive spot deep inside her.

She tightened around him.

He rubbed harder.

Amantha moaned. "Wallaig."

"Such a good lass." Tugging at her folds with his teeth, he played, circling her nub with the tip of his tongue. Another thrust. Two more, harder than the last. Monstrous pressure coiled inside her. Her hips jerked. "Aye, just right. You're perfect, *kazlita*. Everything I've always wanted."

"Oh, please, now. I need it now."

With a hum, he twisted his fingers. "Come, Amantha. Let me hear you scream."

His guttural command unleashed a torrent inside her. White light flashed behind her closed eyelids. The orgasm dragged her up and over, ripping her from the real world. With a high-pitched wail, she hurdled into the next. Here and now ceased to exist. Nothing mattered but Wallaig. The sound of his voice inside her head. His hot mouth against her skin. The stroke of his fingers and lash of his tongue.

Using his teeth, he nipped her gently.

She came again, lost to ecstasy, anchored by nothing but the hard hands holding her up. She heard him groan. Felt him shift, then stand. Amantha whispered his name. He accepted her invitation and, supporting her in his arms, wrapped her legs around him. Surrounded by him, she offered him her lips. He invaded her mouth. Deep. Fast. Brutal. A kiss of a conqueror, a man bent on possession as he set himself against her and pushed inside. Her muscles stretched. She panted in alarm. He didn't give her time to adjust. Showing no mercy, he pressed in, making her take him.

Bending her knee, he pushed her leg up and out, opening her wider. His hips shifted. He slid deeper and—

Another round of bliss blasted through her.

She pulsed around him.

Baring his teeth, Wallaig didn't stop. He took her hard instead. Advance and retreat. His hardness claiming her softness. Letting her know she belonged to him as he made love to her against the shower wall, dragging her toward the ledge until she fell into the abyss, drunk on pleasure.

13

Mist rolled along the ground and over the ruins as Grizgunn flew overhead. A thin line of sunlight burned on the horizon, reaching out to touch jagged cliffs. His scales tingled in warning. He needed to take cover. In the next ten minutes would be best. He could push it to fifteen if pressed for time, but what would be the point? He was already home. A hop, skip and jump away from entering his new lair.

Angling his wings, he circled once, then set down between the ancient church and the crumbling edge of coastline. His dark blue claws curled into the peat moss. Seawater churned on the rocks below, roaring against the stone face, nature's way of throwing a tantrum. The show of temper epitomized his mood—pissed off with an unholy need to punch something.

With a snarl, he bared his fangs and folded his wings. Goddamn the Scot. The red-scaled warrior had been slippery as an eel, injuring two of his crew before slithering into the city, disappearing like a ghost in the night. His brows furrowed. The male's proficiency at hiding presented a problem. One he needed to solve before sunset. Otherwise, he wouldn't get another shot at the warrior. The whoreson would slip beneath his radar—again—and he'd never get his claws on him... or the high-energy female he protected.

Yeah, he'd seen her.

She'd been hard to miss, her aura glowing bright against the Scot's scales before he'd turned tail and run. A smart move, the only one given the precious cargo he carried. Cracking his knuckles, Grizgunn shook his head. Another HE female, the second in as many months. Unprecedented. Shocking too. Females who tapped into the Meridian, drawing power from the source, weren't thick on the ground. A rarity in the world, most Dragonkind males never encountered one. Which made him wonder what the Scottish pack knew that he didn't. Grizgunn rolled his shoulders. Scales ruffled, clicking together like dominos before settling back into place. He frowned. What the hell was he missing?

The question pissed him off.

The idea the Scots held more knowledge worsened his mood.

A low growl erupted from his throat. He shut down the show of fury. Allowing his rage out of its box wouldn't help. He must remain calm and stay focused. His warriors needed him. Had chosen him to lead the Danish pack, for better or worse. Now was no time to lose his patience. Not when he was close to getting what he wanted—Cyprus's head on a pike and the Scottish territory back under his family's control. He'd made a promise to his sire. The pretender would pay for his treachery. He would accept nothing less.

Inhaling deep, Grizgunn doused his temper and shifted forms. Blue scales morphed into human skin. Bowing his head, he stood naked in the shadow of a stone wall and brushed a hand over his shaved head.

Steam rose from his shoulders as he closed his eyes and conjured his clothes. Jeans and a sweatshirt in place, he stomped his feet into boots and, without waiting for his warriors to land behind him, headed toward his new home.

Once a church, the empty shell stood like a stoic solider near the cliff edge. Abandoned by humans. Unloved by historical societies. A relic long forgotten by those in the shire. He didn't care. The disinterest and isolation suited him, providing the perfect place for him to put down roots. The tunnels and living spaces beneath the ruin were almost complete. Another couple of weeks, and the lair would provide all the comfort he required.

Boot soles crunching over a shattered stone path, he walked beneath a broken archway. He kicked a rock out of his way. Fucking hell. It was frustrating. He hated defeat. Despised being outsmarted even more. Success depended on a three-pronged approach: accurate information, a solid strategy and precise execution. He'd managed two of the three tonight. Item three had been blown to shit by the red-scaled whoreson in Edinburgh. The fact a member of Cyprus's pack had outmaneuvered him rubbed him the wrong way.

It should never have happened. He'd had the area locked down.

Clenching his teeth, Grizgunn swallowed a curse. He needed a new way forward, a failsafe plan that would throw the Scottish pack off balance. Footfalls echoing across eight-hundred-year old stone, he strode into the roofless nave. His mind churned as he sorted through possible strategies. A hostage situation might work. Getting his claws on the warrior who'd disappeared in Edinburgh along with the woman would no doubt shake Cyprus's tree. The aloof mother-fucker wouldn't be so nonchalant then.

He flexed his hands. An enemy male to torture for information. A high-energy female for his warriors to enjoy every day. Grizgunn hummed. Excellent plan, but first...

He needed to find the red-scaled male before Cyprus flew to the rescue. A lone dragon was a vulnerable one. Easy to pick off and overpower once cornered. The trick would be bringing the warrior to ground and caging him fast. The second the Scottish pack showed up, Grizgunn would lose his chance. Not a good outcome. So...where had the Scot gone? How had he hidden with so many dragons on his trail? His eyes narrowed. Searching his memory, he thought back, running through the night's events and...

"Shit—the harbour. The ship." Grizgunn cursed under his breath. He should've thought of it sooner. The conclusion made perfect sense. Other than working cranes and the humans on the ground, nothing else had been moving. Nothing but the ocean freighter, light blue hull pushing through the water as the tugboat helped it exit the port. "Smart move."

But not smart enough.

He knew where to look now. An image flashed in his mind's eye. He saw the flag of Norway flying above the stern and right below it, the name of the ship painted in bright white letters.

"Den Skumløse." Jogging up a set of steps, he stopped beside the alter at the front of the church. "Clever way to escape."

A little disconcerting too. The Scot must be determined. Only a strong male would disregard his fear and enter the water. Not that it mattered. Determination only got a warrior so far. Pressing his palms to the altarpiece, Grizgunn glanced skyward. Stars faded as dawn arrived. Discomfort prickled down his spine. His sonar pinged. Multiple sets of paws set down in the yard outside the ruined church wall.

"Hakon," he said, his voice bleeding through mind-speak. *"Get everyone inside. The sun's coming up."*

"Got the door open?"

"Almost. Move your ass."

His XO grunted.

Grizgunn unleashed a wave of magic. The heavy stone topping the altar shifted up and to the side. Stairs came into view. He descended into the darkness, one thing on his mind. He must get to his computer. A few minutes of research would provide what he needed— the ship's route along with its exact location on the ocean. The second he possessed the information, he would be able track Den Skumløse's progress from dawn until dusk. He smiled in anticipation. Come evening the Scot would be in for a surprise, one that would see him captured and the female he guarded warming Grizgunn's bed.

14

More asleep than awake, Wallaig lay flat on his back in the middle of the bed. His chest rose and fell, the rhythm steady, his muscles so loose he floated on a wave of relaxation. Unusual for him. Most days his feet hit the floor before his mind registered the shift. Pure instinct. Complete focus. Zero hesitation. No need to lounge around in order to wake up, but...

He sighed, the soft rumble full of satisfaction.

What a day, a near perfect seven hours of sleep. A rarity for him. Five was the norm, all he needed on a regular basis. But with Amantha beside him, his dragon half settled, happy to stay in the moment instead of rushing into the next. Eyes still closed, his mouth curved. A nice change, one that made him lazy. Now, he didn't want to get up. Hell, scratch that. With her in his arms, he never wanted to move again.

Turning toward her, he brushed his lips over her hair. Soft, luxurious strands caressed his skin, clinging to the stubble on his jaw. Prickles of pleasure shimmered through him. Another sigh escaped him. Gorgeous female. Such a spirited lass. He'd woken her twice during the day, his need for her so great he'd been unable to leave her alone: touching her, loving her, surrounding himself in the warmth of her personality. True to her nature, she'd given all he asked, feeding him without hesitation, filling him so full his fingertips still tingled from the blast of her bio-energy.

His beast stretched in contentment. Magic thrummed through his veins, and Wallaig hummed. Goddess, it felt so good to be full. Over the years, he'd learned to live with the hunger, along with the longing —the constant gnaw of energy greed and never getting enough. In one afternoon, Amantha had banished the ache, aligning with his dragon half, meeting and matching him so well he couldn't believe his good fortune.

Giving her a gentle squeeze, he kissed the top of her head. Worn out by his attentions, Amantha didn't move. Cheek pressed to his chest, one leg nestled between his thighs, she slept like only a well-pleasured female could, lost in dreams and oblivious to world. He wanted to keep it that way. Let her sleep on. Hold her a while longer. Maybe even make love to her again, but...

A rumble of annoyance left his throat.

It sucked to be him. Lounging in bed all evening wasn't part of the plan. He glanced toward the curtains covering the windows. Drawn tight against the sun, the glow of UV rays dimmed around the fabric edges. It wouldn't be long now—forty-five minutes to an hour and the sun would go down. The second dusk arrived he needed to be in full flight, moving east toward the coast. Which meant, time to check in. His commander might be a patient male, but he wouldn't wait much longer.

Calling on the connection he shared with his pack mates, he opened a channel into mind-speak. *"Cyprus."*

"About bloody time." The snarl exploded between his temples, broadcasting his commander's mood. *"Where are you?"*

"On a ship headed for Norway."

Fabric rustled. Something creaked—a bed maybe —the faint sounds coming through the link as Cyprus shifted. *"What happened?"*

"Got myself into a wee bit of trouble in Edinburgh."

"What the hell, Wallaig? You weren't patrolling any- where near Edinburgh last night."

True enough. He'd started the evening on the south-east boundary, patrolling with Kruger. His friend had gone home at the end of the night. He hadn't. *"I made a pit stop in the city."*

"And?"

"I stopped to check on Amantha."

Cyprus cursed. *"Did I not tell you tae leave well enough alone?"*

"I decided something different."

"I'm going tae rip your tail off and shove it up your arse when you get home."

"Good luck with that," he said, chuckling. Hell, a fight sounded like fun. Better than good. Would be all kinds of interesting too. Cyprus might be younger by almost a century, but age didn't matter. The male never disappointed. He fought dirty and always packed a punch. *"What's done is done, Cy. You want to hear the rest or not?"*

"Jesus Christ," his commander growled. *"All right —tell me."*

Without hesitation, Wallaig relayed the details,

leaving nothing out—his decision to leave the letters, his breaking into Amantha's apartment, her reaction to him, his surprise at meeting her...the worry his female carried for Elise. As he talked, Cyprus listened, absorbing the information, behaving the way a skilled commander of warriors should—hearing him out, gathering all the facts before making a determination.

"*The rogues surrounded Elise and Amantha's building?*" Cyprus asked, a frown in his voice.

"*Aye.*"

"*Grizgunn went after her specifically?*"

"*I think he was after Elise, but stumbled onto Amantha instead.*"

"*Fucking hell.*"

"*Aye, and make no mistake. The bastard had the address. He knew what he was after—an HE female.*"

"*Amantha's high-energy?*"

"*In the best possible way,*" he murmured, glancing at the woman asleep in his arms.

Cyprus snorted. "*Do I need to ask where she is now?*"

"*Do you truly wish to know?*"

"*Be careful, Wallaig,*" his commander said, amusement in his tone. "*You hurt her, and Elise will skin you alive.*"

No doubt. Elise might be a sweetheart most of the time, but she possessed the kind of courage most people lacked. A good thing. His commander needed a strong female by his side. A woman more than just capable of standing her ground, but also able to stop Cyprus in his tracks.

"*I'm not going to hurt her, Cy. Amantha is mine.*"

Cyprus drew a sharp breath. "*You're sure?*"

"*She's my mate. No question. I aim to claim her when she's ready.*"

"You've got tae get her home first."

"Which is where you and the lads come in," he said. *"I need back-up. Grizgunn almost had me in Edinburgh. The near win will make him bold. He won't stop. The bastard will keep coming. My guess is he'll fly out at dusk and—"*

"Try tae kill you and take Amantha before you reach the safety of our lair."

"Exactly. We need to set an ambush. Once I leave the ship, I'll make straight for—"

"Amber Cove."

Wallaig growled as the plan took shape. The ragged cliffs and natural rock formations at Amber Cove acted like a labyrinth, moving inland from the coast, forming deep canyons. He loved flying inside the narrow corridors. The topography was a challenge for any dragon to navigate, but for a male who didn't know the terrain, it would prove deadly.

Shifting on the sheets, Wallaig stroked his hand over Amantha's back. Her soft skin settled him as his mind churned, and he stared at the ceiling. Smooth joints. Perfect paint job. As seamless as the strategy forming inside his head. *"We'll use the labyrinth to hem the rogues in. Take them out one at a time."*

"Might work."

"Should work...as long as Grizgunn takes the bait."

Cyprus grunted. *"You comfortable with that?"*

"Nay." Not even a little. Wallaig clenched his teeth. *"I donnae want Amantha anywhere near the fighting. She's already had one close call today."*

"Grizgunn won't take the bait until he sees her with you," Cyprus said, a wealth of caution in his words. *"For the ambush tae work, he needs tae follow you into the labyrinth."*

"I know," he said, dread pooling in the pit of his stomach.

"Speak with her, Wallaig. Be honest, tell her the whole truth. Trust your mate tae be strong enough tae be part of our pack...tae help eliminate our enemies."

Easier said than done. He hated the idea of her in danger. His beast raged, refusing to contemplate using her as bait. But as Cyprus continued to talk, laying out the rest of the plan, Wallaig couldn't argue with him. The strategy held all the hallmarks of a successful mission. One small problem: the female he didn't wish to risk, and now knew he couldn't live without. Too bad opportunity waited for no one. He held the chance to eliminate the Danish pack in the palm of his hand, so...

No real choice at all.

Like it or not, he must take his commander's advice. Be honest. Tell Amantha everything, then trust her to make a decision that would affect the entire Scottish pack. Hugging her tighter, Wallaig glanced at the curtains again. Weak light bled around the fabric edges. He didn't have much time. The sun continued its descent, dipping low on the horizon as the ship powered over rolling waves.

The subtle motion seeped into his bones.

Wallaig closed his eyes and turned toward Amantha. He traced the arch of her eyebrow. Caressed the curve of her cheek. The need to protect her chased desire through his veins. Drawing a fortifying breath, he kissed the tip of her nose. So beautiful. So trusting in his arms. His mate, a true gift from the goddess.

With a murmur, he stroked her bottom. Goose bumps pebbled on her skin. She grumbled, then stretched, murmuring his name as her legs slid against his. Kissing her gently, he sent a prayer heavenward, asking the Goddess of All Things for guidance. He needed to find the right words, a way to explain

without frightening her. The last thing he wanted was
for her to run scared. A distinct possibility when she
learned the plan—that she was about to become the
bait in a game of cat and mouse designed to catch a
monster.

15

S tanding on the deck of the ship beside Wallaig, Amantha gripped his hand and wondered when she'd gone crazy. Sometime in the last twelve hours for sure. Nothing else explained the lengths she wanted to go for him—or what she was about to do at his request.

The words *dragon bait* banged around inside her head.

Her throat tightened. Mère de Dieu, she must be out of her ever-loving mind.

Taking a deep breath, she looked out over the ocean. Dark waves crested beneath a shadowed moon, then disappeared beneath the bow of the ship. The pitch and roll mimicked her mood, steady one minute, chaotic the next. Her stomach lurched as she turned to the man-dragon by her side. Wallaig met her gaze, his damaged eyes shimmering a strange gold-green in the moonlight. She drew another breath, trying to control her disquiet. With a murmur, he cupped her cheek, the caress so gentle tears clogged her throat. After spending the day with him, she knew his touch, now craved his closeness, longed for the comfort he provided with nothing more than the stroke of his fingertips.

A weird thing to admit.

She'd met him less than twenty-four hours ago, and yet, felt him with every breath she took. Her reaction wasn't logical. She didn't want it to be—she wanted this, him and the bond tethering her to him. She guessed that explained why she stood on a freighter in the middle of the English Channel about to do something foolish. All to ensure Wallaig got what he needed. What his family—dragon pack... whatever—required to stay safe.

He'd sat her down less than an hour ago and explained the situation...taken the time to talk it through. So much appreciated. She liked that he didn't mince words. He was honest and straightforward, refusing to hide from her. Now, she knew more than she wanted to about Dragonkind and the rogue pack in his territory. Her brow furrowed. No, not true. She was lying to herself. She didn't know more about Wallaig than she could handle. The dragon stuff seemed scary, but once curiosity took hold she hadn't been shy. She'd asked question after question, wanting to know more, needing to know everything, unable to hear enough about his life. All the while wondering where she fit in...and if her heart was right when it insisted she belonged next to him.

"All right, lass?"

"Not really," she whispered, feeling like an idiot, yearning for reassurance. So much for courage. She kept telling herself to be brave, but somehow, fear kept resurfacing, threatening to drag her under. "I need a hug before we go."

"*Kazlita.*" Wrapping his arms around her, he pulled

her in tight. His body warmed her. His scent surrounded her, bringing much-needed relief, allowing her to take a full breath. "Please, donnae worry."

"You always call me that. What does it mean?"

"Fierce one."

She huffed. "In your language?"

"Aye—Dragonese."

"Well, it's lovely, but..." Burrowing deeper into his arms, she pressed her nose to his chest. "I'm not feeling very fierce right now."

"Completely normal. You are new to Dragonkind. You donnae know what to expect, but I do," he said, rubbing her back. "I know exactly how it's going to go. Donnae be afraid, lass. I'll be with you every step of the way. I will keep you safe."

She nodded. "Okay. Let's go...before I lose my nerve."

He smiled against the top of her head. "Impossible. You are braver than you believe."

"Maybe," she said, his faith in her waking something deep inside her. Something long dormant, and as her heart came alive, cracking open, grabbing hold of him, Amantha swallowed the lump in her throat. She didn't understand it, but what Wallaig thought of her mattered. She needed him to value her—to want her, no matter what happened in the next few hours. "I did threaten you with a rolling pin, after all."

He snorted. "You clubbed me with it."

"You deserved it."

"Aye, and so much more," he said, his voice guttural. "Lass?"

"Yeah?"

"I want you—today, tomorrow...forever and always. Never doubt it."

His pronouncement startled her. She jerked against him. "You can't know that."

"I can." With a quick pivot, he trapped her between his body and the railing. "Now is not the time to speak of it, but know this—you are my mate, Amantha. *Mine.* So you'd best get used to me fast, lass. I'm keeping you."

The thrill of being claimed grabbed hold. Hope invaded her heart. The independent woman inside her stomped on it. "I'm not a pair of shoes, Wallaig. You can't just decide to—"

"Sure, I can. Now, hang on." Without warning, he shifted into a dragon.

Hard scales brushed her cheek. She screeched like a sissy. "Merde! A little warning next time, please."

Baring huge fangs, Wallaig laughed and shook his head.

Surprised she wasn't afraid, she set her hands on her hips and glared up at him.

"And she thinks she isnae brave," he said more to himself, than to her.

She scowled. "Listen—"

"Later, lass. Time to go. We've work to do."

An enormous paw tipped by black claws reached for her. Amantha braced for contact. His blood-red talon came around her. An instant later, she landed on his back. With a shift of his massive bulk, he settled her between the spikes on his shoulder blades. Invisible tethers wrapped over the tops of her thighs, ensuring she stayed in place. He murmured, telling her to hold on, then unfurled his wings and leapt off the ship.

Her stomach dipped.

Cold air cracked against her skin a second before a warm bubble closed around her. Protected from the wind, riding Wallaig into the unknown, exhilaration took hold. Amantha whooped as he spiralled upward, entering the night sky, making her forget she was headed into dragon battle with nothing but a pair of invisible leg straps—and absolutely no safety net.

16

E nergy pulsed in the air around him, lighting up the sky like aurora borealis. Reddish-pink shimmered into greenish-gold. A pretty sight any other night, but as Wallaig rocketed out of the clouds, white contrails streaming from his wingtips, he didn't give a fuck about the light show. He was hunting rogue. He needed a heat signature, an energy blip on the horizon—something, anything to indicate the enemy knew he was coming.

He hoped to hell that wasn't the case.

The element of surprise always worked in a dragon favor. But after the clusterfuck of the last twelve hours, he refused to take anything for granted. Not with Amantha on his back and a potential firefight in his future.

Speed supersonic, he scanning the horizon above the distance shore. Ten miles out, the craggy coastline rose like a spectre in the dark and...all clear so far. Wallaig prayed it stayed that way. He could use a little all-calm-on-the-Scottish-front tonight.

Making sure he hadn't missed anything, he surveyed the terrain again. White cliffs rose against the night sky, standing strong against churning surf and surging seas. With each rolling assault, water crashed against the rocks, spraying mist sky high. The smell of brine swirled in the air, mixing with the scent of coming snow.

Amantha shifted on his back.

He tapped into her bio-energy, checking to see if she was all right. The Meriden reacted, opening a channel. Potent and powerful, the current Amantha carried reached out to stroke him. Wallaig hummed as her emotion grid popped up on his mental screen. He exhaled in relief. All good. Still steady. Riding high as she followed his flight corrections.

Gripping the spikes behind his horns, she leaned left and shifted right when he did, adjusting to his movements, flying like a pro. Happiness burned through him, blurring the lines, making him forget the mission for a moment.

Goddess, she made him proud.

Despite her fear, she stayed the course, refusing to back down. No tears or hysterics for his lass. Just stone-cold courage in the face of adversity. His beast purred in appreciation. Her intelligence and quick wit, the determination she showed—everything about her delighted him. His mouth curved. He must have been born under a lucky star...or with a horseshoe up his arse. He didn't care which reason applied. He'd take it and run...as long as it meant he got to keep her in the end.

By no means a sure thing.

Wallaig knew it. No matter how powerful, energy-fuse wasn't a cure-all. The magical bond between mates pulled couples together, but it didn't keep them that way. Healthy relationships took time to grow, needing care and nurturing along the way. Which meant he still had work to do. His dragon might have chosen Amantha, but he needed her to choose him back. Nothing short of wholehearted consent would do, so...how should he proceed? Push or pull. Chase or allow her to come to him. Sad to say, but he didn't know.

The confusion left him reeling. Uncertainty wasn't a strong position, but the fact remained—he couldn't force the connection. Amantha needed to make up her own mind about him. Accept or reject him. Be his mate or not. Walk away or stay forever.

Nerves hit him like a body shot. So much at stake. Too much to lose. Somehow, some way, he must convince Amantha to give him a chance. So far, he hadn't given her much reason to stay with him. From the moment he broke into her apartment—and scared her half to death—he'd made one mistake after another. Not very romantic. If he could go back, he would do it differently. Wine and dined her. Treated her like a princess. Taken her out on the town and shown her a good time.

A lovely thought. An even better idea, but well... shite. He'd already blown his shot at making a good first impression.

As it stood now, the only bright spot in a long line of disasters was her desire for him. He felt it with every breath he took. Drank in her need, sensed her longing even as he suffered from his own. His female might not understand why she reacted to him the way she did, but bond he shared with her was strong. Almost unbreakable even after a few hours. The sharpness of her reaction to him told him she wasn't immune. Which gave him hope and...made him feel like a jerk.

Seven miles out now, Wallaig levelled out over the water. He wasn't being fair to her. She deserved the whole truth, not the bits and pieces he'd given her. Aye, she knew a lot about Dragonkind now, but nothing about energy-fuse. Selfish of him, but...God smite him dead with a thunderbolt. He hadn't wanted to chance it.

He longed for Amantha too much to risk her rejection. Not yet. Not so soon after meeting her. She needed time to come to know him. He needed time to convince her, so...screw transparency. Throw conventional thinking into a deep, dark hole. He would tell her when she needed to know, and not a moment before he was ready.

Inhaling deep, Wallaig exhaled slow and, tightening his control, tucked the problem away to deal with another night. Now was no time for distraction.

Attention locked on the cliffs, he located his entry point. Six miles ahead, a hair north of his position, the mouth of the canyon lay tucked behind a jut-out on the coastline. Searching for movement along the rocks, he sent out an exploratory ping. Inferno-like heat expanded in his veins. He hung onto the power, allowed it to burn higher and hotter, then released it. The rush tumbled out in front of him, blanketing the water before hitting land. Like the giant wave, the fury of his magic splashed up and over, settling over the terrain, feeding him information.

Five miles out and closing fast.

Fine-tuning his sonar, Wallaig reached out to his pack. *"Lads—I'm here."*

Kruger growled in greeting.

"Time to target?" Levin asked, his tone full of predatory intent.

"Forty-five seconds," he said, coming up on the three-mile marker. The instant he broke through the

barrier, the rogues would be able to detect him. *"Get ready."*

"We're good tae go…hidden amid the cliffs inside the labyrinth," Tydrin murmured, the scrape of sharp claws over rock coming through mind-speak.

"Keep tae the plan." Scales clicked as Cyprus shifted, preparing to take flight. *"The second Grizgunn and his pack enter the canyon behind you, bug out."*

"Got it."

"I'm serious, Wallaig," Cyprus said, the mistrust in his tone telling. *"Protect your female and head for the lair. No heroics."*

Wallaig bared his fangs. Cold air blasted over his teeth and…bloody ever-lasting hell. He hated the fucking plan—absolutely despised the idea of leaving his brothers-in-arms behind to fight while he flew home. As the eldest of the Scottish pack, he led more than he followed. Duty dictated the path. Honor held sway over the rest, making him the first warrior into battle, and the one last out. But not tonight. His commander was right. He needed to take a backseat and let his pack mates lead the way.

A hard truth to face.

He did it anyway. Screw his pride. Forget about the desire to fight. Both needed to go on the back burner. He must protect his mate. Amantha was too precious to risk, more important than the momentary pleasure of cracking Grizgunn's skull.

The thought centered him.

"No heroics," he murmured, flexing his talons. *"But Cy?"*

"Aye."

"Donnae miss."

"I willnae, brother. I'm going tae rip Grizgunn's guts out and tie a bow beneath his chin."

He huffed. Well, all right then. Good enough. No need to doubt his friend's commitment to the coming violence.

Adjusting his trajectory, Wallaig blew past the three-mile marker. "Amantha."

"I'm ready," she said, tightening her grip on him.

Nay, she wasn't. Never would be either, but he refused to argue. "Stay low, lass. I want you pressed right up against my scales—got it?"

Amantha didn't answer. She obeyed instead. Shifting forward, she laid down flat, pressing her belly and chest to his spine. Her cheek met his scales. She found new handholds, flexing her fingers around spikes behind his horns. Scanning the cliffs again, he increased his wing-speed and descended another one hundred feet. Whitecaps rolled beneath him, kicking up spray, coating his interlocking dragon skin with salt and sea.

The distance between him and the coast closed, bringing him within range.

His eyes narrowed, he hunted for a flash of blue on rocky outcroppings. He knew Grizgunn lay in wait. With his magic up and running, he detected multiple rogues in the vicinity, but needed the males to move. The second one of them shifted, the magical displacement would cause a chain reaction and light up his radar, allowing him to see the bastards in the dark.

A great strategy. One tiny problem.

The longer the enemy remained patient—and still —the closer Wallaig would be when the rogues took flight. Less distance to target equaled little time to react, making close quarters claw-to-claw combat a real possibility before he reached the canyon.

Smart of Grizgunn.

Bad for him.

Understanding dawned. Bloody hell. The bastards were reeling him in. Planned to tag him on the rocks and cut him off—bring him to ground—before his brothers-in-arms exited the canyon.

With a curse, Wallaig banked away from the coastline. The webbing on his wings caught air. His muscles stretched, threatening to rip as he changed direction. Pain tore across his rib cage. Wallaig didn't care. Ignoring the claw of discomfort, he pushed harder, plotting a new trajectory. He needed to find a different entry point into the labyrinth, somewhere north of his position before—

His sonar pinged.

Movement flashed along the cliff edge.

Wallaig growled as enemy dragons left their hidey-holes. Rogues at two, six and three o'clock, wings spread wide, already in the sky. As he watched, the rogue pack organized in mid-air, forming three fighting triangles, killing all hope of him making it into the labyrinth.

"*Goddamn it.*" Wallaig turned north. His wingtip dipped into the water, making him wobble. He snarled, tore free of the ocean surf, and increased his velocity. "*Cyprus—primary point of access no longer an option. Too many rogues for me to fly through.*"

"*How many?*"

"*Nine warriors. Three fighting triangles.*"

Cyprus cursed.

"*On my way,*" Levin growled, wings already flapping. "*Your plan?*"

"*Head north. Use the stone towers along the coast as cover. The mist is always heavy there. I'll lose'em in the tall rocks.*" Looking over his shoulder, he checked the rogues' position. Less than a quarter of a mile away. Too fucking close. Another couple hundred yards, and the bastards would be within range. Close enough to exhale and unleash the fury of a fireball. Not good news for him. Even worse news for his mate. His scales would protect him from a barrage of fire and acid, but Amantha's skin wouldn't withstand the onslaught. She'd be burned alive, reduced to nothing but ash on top of his back. *"Move yer arses, lads. I've got a pack of rogues on my tail."*

Attuned to his pack, he sensed his brothers-in-arms take flight. The warriors split into two groups: Levin and Kruger flew north to intercept him. Cyprus, Rannock and Tydrin took a wider path, hoping to sneak in behind Grizgunn and divide the enemy's attention.

"Hold on, Wallaig," Rannock said, calm even in the face of a clusterfuck.

Kruger snarled, seconding the sentiment. *"We're coming."*

Not fast enough. He needed back-up now. Before the rogues caught up, and he lost his female in the fray.

17

Flying fast between huge standing stones, Wallaig dodged right, then banked left, diving behind a jagged column jutting up from the sea floor. Nipping at his heels, the yellow dragon hissed behind him. He risked a quick glance over his shoulder. A set of fangs flashed a second before flames flared in his periphery. The air warped. Blistering heat nipped the tip of his tail. The multi-headed spikes along his spine rattled as he roared around another rock formation and—

Boom!

The fireball slammed into the cliff above his head.

The rock face shattered. Shards rained down, pelting him with shrapnel.

Amantha called his name.

Tightening the shield protecting her, he murmured, hoping to calm her. A long shot, but...shite. Anything was better than feeling the chaotic spike of her bio-energy. Her emotion grid indicated fear. She was panicking, heart thumping hard, breathing too fast, her palms so sweaty she kept losing her grip on him.

Wallaig growled as rage too hold. Goddamn the rogues. He wanted to whip around and nail the warrior shadowing him through the rocky maze along the coastline. Not to save himself, but to spare Amantha. He couldn't stand her pain. Hated the situation along with the necessity of bringing her to this point. And as anger on her behalf tipped into aggression, Wallaig fought to maintain control. The need to rip the yellow-scaled arsehole limb from limb coursed through him.

His mind supplied the details of the kill.

Weaving in and out, he faked right and flew left. The rogue stayed with him, dogging his every move. An imagine took shape and form inside his head. He pictured the bastard's blood on his claws, heard the screams as he grabbed the warrior's horns and tore his skull in two.

Christ, but he wanted to do it. Turn the tide. Fight instead of flee. Kill instead of evade. Only one thing kept him from it—Amantha. He didn't want her to see the bloodbath, never mind get any smeared on her skin. His mate deserved better from him. Was too fine to be touched by such filth, so instead of fighting, he whirled around a rock face and, cutting through thick mist, searched for a way to stay ahead of enemy claws.

Rounding a bend, he reached toward an outcropping. The sharp tips of his talons scraped over stone. A huge boulder broke away from the stone wall. Gripping it like a baseball, he spun around the next curve. White trails whistling off his wingtips, he sensed the rogue following.

"Come on. Come on," he murmured, waiting for the male to poke his nose around the bend.

A white and yellow dragon snout appeared.

Baring his fangs, Wallaig somersaulted up and over. Halfway through the rotation, he launched the weapon. The huge rock hurtled through the air. Pale scales shimmering in the lowlight, the male squawked, tried to adjust, but—

Bull's-eye.

The boulder slammed into his head.

Yellow scales blurred as the rogue's neck whiplashed. His skull slammed into the side of the cliff. Stunned by the blow, the warrior hung in mid-air, struggling to stay airborne.

Kruger snarled his name.

Flipping sideways, Wallaig ducked. Green, black-tipped scales flashed in the moonlight. A bladed tailed whipped past as Kruger dove over top of him. Dark gaze glowing with demonic light, his friend grabbed the rogue by the horns. Spinning full circle, his pack mate gouged the enemy. Black claws pushed into the male's eye sockets. Dragon blood sprayed up Kruger's forearms as he punched through the yellow dragon's skull. The warrior screamed. Kruger showed no mercy, and with a quick twist, snapped his neck. As the bastard died, his corpse turned to ash, sending a flurry of grey flakes into the air.

Flicking flecks from his claws, Kruger glanced his way. *"Go, brother."*

"Aye. Get her out of here." Blue, grey and gold tiger stripped scales streaked into view as Levin rocketed over the cliff edge. *"We'll hold the line until you're safely away."*

Whirling around, Wallaig took his friend's advice. *"Watch yer six, lads. There are more out there."*

Eager for another fight, Kruger cracked his knuckles.

Levin hissed in challenge as three rogues careened around a stone column.

Already in retreat, Wallaig heard the crack of claws against scales behind him, but didn't turn around. No sense going back…or worrying about his friends. He knew from experience Levin and Kruger had the enemy in hand. Fast in flight, lethal in a fight, the pair worked well together. Even when outnumbered, the warriors wreaked havoc, delivering a double-edge assault most couldn't withstand. And as the duo covered his escape, ensuring he got Amantha out in one piece, Wallaig thanked the goddess for his friends.

Most males would've saved their own skins.

Not his brothers-in arms. His pack held the line, watching his back as he left the cliffs behind and flew hard for home.

Coastline turned to farmer fields, then gave way to city lights and suburban streets. On the outskirts of Aberdeen, Wallaig circled west. Mountains loomed in the distance as he slowed to a glide on the edge of town. Small houses and narrow streets flowed into granite clad buildings surrounded by wider boulevards. The sky rumbled overhead. The first raindrop struck. Half snow, half water, slush slid over his scales as he spotted the pub on Embers Street.

Owned by the Scottish pack, the Dragon's Horn—and the century old whiskey distillery behind it—took up three city blocks. Thick stone walls rose around the property, providing privacy while keeping unwanted visitors out. A little patch of heaven protected by magic in the center of the city. Nice and neat. Clean and tidy. The perfect place for dragons to hide in plain view, and precisely where he needed to land.

Zeroing in on the large courtyard behind the pub, Wallaig folded his wings. Gravity took hold, pulling him out of the sky. His back paws thumped down. His fore claws followed, scraping over stone tile a second before he reached around and pulled Amantha off his back.

Quivering in his paw, she wheezed, struggling to breathe.

Shite. Not good. She was past panic, more than upset. Close now to hyperventilating and—

Needing to touch her with his hands, Wallaig shifted into human form. Wrapping her in his arms, he pulled her into his chest. "Shh, *kazlita*, shh. It's all right. You're all right."

She shook her head. "I can't breathe. I c-can't catch my breath. I'm—"

"I've got you," he said, repeating it over and over as he picked her up and strode across the courtyard. Cradling her in his arms, he bypassed the fountain featuring a three-headed snake, stepped onto the porch, and sat down on a wooden bench. Rain pattered against the roof above his head. Wallaig arranged her in his lap, setting her astride him, pulling her close, letting her feel the warmth of his skin. "Breathe, lass. I've got you."

"Wallaig." With a small cry, she clutched at him. "Those dragons were so scary, and…G-god, the fireball. It nearly h-hit us."

"I know, but it's over now," he murmured, caressing her back, hating the scent of her fear. "We're home, Amantha. You're safe. The bastards cannae track us here."

"Are you sure?"

"Aye."

Her head tucked beneath his chin, she shuddered against him.

He kept talking, praising her courage, telling her

how proud she made him, using the steady rhythm of his voice to help calm her. Seconds passed into minutes. Pressing her face to the side of his throat, Amantha started to breathe easier. One stilted inhale turned into deeper ones and...miracle of miracles, the strategy seemed to work. The more he talked, the more she relaxed. Another shiver shook her. He upped his game, deepening his voice, caressing her with gentle hands and soft words. Little by little, the tension drained from her muscles, leaving her soft and pliant in his arms.

"Sweet lass. You were so brave."

"Wallaig?"

"Uh-huh."

"Are you okay?" she asked, tone soft with concern. Her hand moved over his arm, checking for scrapes.

His chest went tight. Precious wee lass. Her fear for him cracked him wide open. Love poured out, filling him so full he couldn't contain it. Stroking her hair, he cleared his throat. "A few bumps and bruises. Naught to worry about, lass."

"Okay, good, but..." As she trailed off, he angled his head to better view her face. Eyes closed, a frown marring her brow, Amantha pressed her cheek against his chest. "Can we not do that ever again?"

"Never again, *kazlita*," he said, kissing her temple. "I swear on my life—never again."

His vow to keep her safe spiralled into the open air, joining the drum of rain on the roof. Amantha sighed as the last of her fear faded. She snuggled closer. He hugged her tighter, content to hold and keep her warm, unwilling to rush her inside. The night was only half over. He had plenty of time. All he wanted to do now was ensure her comfort.

The rest would follow.

Tomorrow would be soon enough to show her what she meant to him. His strategy was simple: keep his word and win her heart. He'd already given her fair warning. She knew he planned to keep her. Now, all he needed to do was convince her to stay.

18

Standing in the kitchen inside the underground lair, Amantha plucked a chocolate truffle off a glass tray. Careful not to crush it, she dropped the ball into a bowl of dark cocoa powder. A quick roll. A light dusting. Just the right amount of bitter coating the sweet, and she fished it out, set it on a piece of wax paper, and picked up the next.

Pursing her lips, she surveyed her choices. Dunk it in cocoa again or—

With a hum, she rolled the treat in a dish full of finely chopped nuts. Two down, twenty-three left to smother in the topping of her choice. Her mouth curved, she swayed to the song on the radio as she worked. Contentment swamped her. She loved her new home. Practically worshiped the kitchen inside the underground lair, even though it didn't have a chilled section of countertop to roll out pastry dough. The layout wasn't perfect for a bakery, not by a long shot, but she adored it anyway.

The richness of Cherrywood cupboards, the smooth Carrara countertops, the fancy mouldings and high-tech appliances made her feel at home. As though she'd found her place and belonged where she stood—inside a secret lair with a bunch of dragon warriors...all of whom suffered from a serious sweet tooth.

Amantha huffed in amusement.

Sitting on the other side of the island, Elise looked up from her book. "What's so funny?"

"Just thinking about Wallaig's reaction to lemon tarts."

Her friend raised a brow. "Explosive?"

"Orgasmic," she murmured, the memory of him smearing creamy filling on her skin making her shiver. He'd taken his time licking it off, leaving no part of her untouched. "For me."

"I love reciprocation," Elise said, flipping a page in her book. "I read to Cyprus from an ancient Bedouin text the other night. I couldn't walk straight the next day."

Amantha snorted. "Steamy stuff?"

Blue eyes sparkling, her friend grinned. "It had concubines in it."

"You are such a tease."

"Can't help it." Color rising in her face, Elise shrugged. "I want him all the time. It's a little embarrassing."

She knew the feeling. Three weeks to the day of her rescue, and she couldn't get enough of Wallaig either. She thought about him all the time. Worried about him when he left the lair. Enjoyed every moment he spent with her inside it. Which ended up being a lot. If he was home, he was with her. Well...she frowned...except for this afternoon.

Rolling a truffle in colorful sprinkles, she shook her head. No doubt in her mind. He was up to something. A creature of habit, he never changed his routine. Today, though, he'd sidestepped questions and skipped out early, leaving her to the truffles, making her suspicious. Now, she wondered what the heck he had planned. Something sneaky. Something interesting. Something to do with her, for sure.

"Elise?"

"Yup."

"What's going on?"

"What do you mean?" Elise went all wide-eyed, a sure sign of treachery.

Amantha scowled. "Don't give me that. You know what I mean. Where did the guys go?"

"Can't tell you." Completely unrepentant, Elise snapped her book closed. "I crossed my heart and hoped to die, so—"

"You suck. Girls are supposed to stick together."

"Not this time. And anyway..." Her friend tilted her head as a tingle swept the back of Amantha's neck. "You're about to find out. The guys are home."

Brushing cocoa powder off her fingertips, Amantha tugged on her apron strings. The knot loosened as heavy footfalls approached the kitchen. Tossing the apron onto a nearby stool, she turned toward the entrance just as Wallaig pushed open the door. Wraparounds in place, his gaze met hers. Butterflies took flight in the pit of her stomach. Prickles ghosted over her skin and...God. He always did that to her. Her reaction bordered on insane. No matter how many times she laid eyes on him he made her body sing and her heart yearn.

"*Kazlita*," he said, the rumble in his voice making her quiver.

"Hi," she whispered, acting like a green girl, instead of the woman he made love to every day. "Want a truffle?"

Her voice pulled him across the kitchen. "Is it lemon flavored?"

Her lips twitched. God help her, he was obsessed. Looked as though she'd be making more lemon tarts later. Thank God. "No, chocolate."

"Leave them to Levin, then," he said. "That annoying SOB loves chocolate."

Skirting the island, Wallaig stopped in front of her. Unable to resist, she flattened her hands on his chest and tipped her chin up, asking without words for a kiss. With a hum, he dipped his head. Big hands playing in her hair, he brushed his mouth over hers. One gentle kiss, a quick flick of his tongue and he withdrew, leaving her wanting.

She protested with a murmur.

He nipped her bottom lip. "Patience, lass. We've time and more for loving later. But first, come with me. I have a surprise for you."

"What is it?"

He snorted. "Well, now, it wouldn't be much of a surprise if I told you."

True enough. "I've never been one for surprises, Wallaig."

"Trust me, Amantha." The corners of his eyes crinkled behind his wraparounds. "You'll like this one."

Stepping back, he held out his hand. She took it without hesitation, allowing him to lead her out of the kitchen. Excitement kicked in as he towed her across the main living area. Footfalls muffled by plush Turkish rugs, he skirted the couches and wide-backed chairs sitting beneath the colorful stained-glass ceiling and headed for the staircase across the room. Lacing her fingers with his, she climbed the stairs and stepped into a large vestibule.

Scarred in places, a wide wooden door stood across the space.

She glanced at Wallaig. "We're going into the pub?"

"Aye." Tugging on her hand, he drew her forward. As he opened the door, jazz music poured into the vestibule, the mournful song of a lone saxophone. "Or rather, through it."

Huh. Okay. If he hadn't had her attention before, he did now.

Curiosity running rampant, Amantha followed him into the tavern. More high-end restaurant than pub, the wall-to-wall wood panelling and coffered ceiling should've made the space feel dark. Somehow, though, it didn't. The décor screamed old world instead: comfortable, intimate and cozy in a way she appreciated. Her gaze drifted over patrons seated in plush booths and clustered around large tables with comfortable chairs. Her mouth curved. Not an empty seat in the house. Rannock would be pleased by the turnout.

In charge of the whiskey distillery and restaurant, the huge warrior stood behind the bar mixing drinks...trying not to glare at Levin. Golden eyes full of mischief, Levin shoved Rannock to one side and grabbed a bottle of wine. The warrior pushed him back. Levin said something she couldn't hear. As the men tussled behind the bar, Wallaig shook his head at their antics, but didn't stop to talk. Pace steady, he passed the swinging kitchen doors, made a sharp left, and walked toward another door.

A second before he reached it, the wooden panel swung open.

Amantha followed him over the threshold in to a bright space. She glanced around. Plaster walls painted pale yellow. A wide expanse of windows fronting the street to her right. Tin panels stamped with a pretty pattern over her head, absolutely no furniture and…two big boxes sitting in the center of the room.

She read the writing on the side of the cardboard. Her breath caught. "Stoves?"

"Commercial grade. Rannock assures me they are the very best."

"You're giving me ovens?"

"Nay, Amantha," he murmured, taking off his sunglasses. His damaged eyes met hers, holding her secure. "I'm giving you a bakery. The shop is yours, to do with as you please. A construction crew will be here on the morrow to see to any renovations."

Shock bombarded her. Her mind spun as she looked around. Amantha sucked in a breath as the enormity of his surprise hit her. "Oh, my God. This is my dream, Wallaig. It's my *dream*. You…I can't believe…it's beyond anything, so perfect and…"

Her voice cracked. Tears filled her eyes.

"*Kazlita.*"

Overcome by his generosity, she turned and launched herself at him. He caught her with a grunt. Wrapping her arms around him, she whispered, "Thank you. Thank you…oh, my God, thank you. It's an incredible gift. The best surprise—thank you!"

"I love you, Amantha," he said against the top of her head. "I want you to be happy here."

Her heart paused mid-beat, then thumped hard. "You love me?"

"Aye…with all that I am."

Awe whipped through her, making happiness rise. "I love you too."

"Thank Christ."

"You were worried?"

"A little," Tucking a strand of hair behind her ear, he rested his forehead against hers. "The fall has been hard and fast for us, lass. I wasn't sure—"

"Never doubt my love, Wallaig—never." Cupping his jaw, she kissed him softly. "I feel as though I've been waiting a lifetime for you. Waiting to tell you how much I need you...how much I want you...how much I love you."

With a groan, he deepened the kiss, his urgency easy to read. She didn't deny him. Amantha welcomed him with all of her heart, knowing she would never let him go. Wallaig was hers. Through no small miracle, she now belonged to him. No matter what the future brought, she would face it head-on, secure in the knowledge he would keep her safe and love her until the end of time.

EPILOGUE

Maps tucked under his arm, a bowl of pasta in his hand, Grizgunn walked into the common room. Five stories below the abandoned church, the natural cave served as the hub inside his new lair. A huge find. Such a great space. His warriors had made quick work of digging hallways off the subterranean cavern. Now three corridors stretched from the main area to reach bedroom suites carved into solid rock.

Glancing up at the light globes bobbing against the curved ceiling, he smiled. A recent addition, the magic-driven illumination negated the need for candles. Not a moment too soon either. He needed the extra light today. Flying out of the lair unprepared again wasn't an option. Fucking Scottish pack. The whoresons were like cats—the warriors kept landing on their feet. So annoying. Beyond frustrating, but after what he'd witnessed on the coast a month ago, not entirely unexpected. Cyprus wasn't an idiot. More's the pity. Neither were the males he commanded, so...

Time to do some studying.

No way would he leave the lair unprepared again.

Skirting a wheelbarrow, Grizgunn stepped around a stack of paint cans and headed for the large table in the center of the room. The smell of wet plaster on newly scored walls drifted in the air. With a grunt, he pulled the drop cloth off the massive oak slab and tossed the roll of maps onto the clean surface. The coiled paper unrolled with a snap as he shifted the bowl to his other hand and shovelled some penne into his mouth. The sharp tang of tomato sauce exploded across his taste buds. He chewed, took another bite and began perusing the top chart.

Stolen from a geographical society in Edinburgh, the map provided details of the British coast. Every inlet and jut-out, each cliff and all the canyons Cyprus had used to evade him the night he missed his chance to capture a high value target. The loss of the red-scaled male had been bad enough, but failing to nab the high-energy female was a real blow. His pack needed someone like her, a female powerful enough to keep his warriors entertained and well-fed.

Clenching his teeth, Grizgunn ran his finger over the map, committing the coastline to memory. He spooned more pasta into his mouth.

Heavy footfalls sounded behind him.

Straightening away from the table, Grizgunn glanced over his shoulder. "Good eve, Hakon."

"Hey," Hakon mumbled around a mouthful of supper. Bowl in hand, his friend crossed the room. Grabbing a chair on the way by, he dragged it over to the table edge, sat down, and put his feet up. As his boots hit the polished oak top, his XO finished chewing. "Got some news."

"Anything good?"

"Depends."

Grizgunn raised a brow. "On what?"

"Whether or not it's true."

"Tell me."

Shifting in his seat, Hakon played with his food, shoving noodles around the bowl with his fork. "There is a Scottish warrior in Prague."

"Alone?" he asked, his interest sharpening. A lone warrior was a vulnerable one—easily brought down by a pack if cornered. Most warriors flew in groups of two or three for just that reason. "Any connection to Cyprus?"

"Rumor has it, his brother." A predatory light in his pale eyes, Hakon smiled, all teeth, no mercy. "His blood brother—a twin, a male by the name of Vyroth."

"Jesus Christ," Setting his bowl down with a thump, Grizgunn leaned against the table and stared at his friend. "Who do we have in Prague?"

"No one loyal to us, but..." His eyes narrowed, Hakon tipped his head back. And Grizgunn waited. He knew that look: concentration multiplied by a thousand and deviousness times a million. Whenever his XO wore it, good things happened. "Montgomery lives there."

"Do you trust him?"

Hakon shrugged. "As much as anyone does a mercenary. Pay him enough money though, and he'll get the job done."

Grizgunn flexed his hands. Money wasn't a problem. His pack possessed plenty: gold, silver, precious artifacts, and enough cash to finance the next world war, so...new strategy. He might have missed his chance at the red-scaled whoreson, but he wouldn't fuck this one up. Cyprus had a twin, a blood brother out alone in the world. A sitting duck just waiting to be plucked. A male he could use as leverage to bring the Scottish pack to heel. Rolling his shoulders, he cracked his knuckles. Nothing left to do now but set his plan in motion and have Vyroth delivered to his doorstep...in chains.

A NOTE FROM THE AUTHOR

Thank you for taking the time to read Fury of a Highland Dragon. If you enjoyed it, please help others find my books so they can enjoy them too.

Recommend it: Please help other readers find this book by recommending it to friends, readers' groups, and discussion boards.

Review it: Let other readers know what you liked or didn't like about Fury of a Highland Dragon.

Lend it: This e-book is lending-enabled, so feel free to share it with your friends. Sign up for my newsletter to receive new release information and other freebies. You can follow me on Facebook or on Twitter under @coreenecallahan.

Book updates can be found at www.CoreeneCallahan.com

Thanks again for taking the time to read my books!

ALSO BY COREENE CALLAHAN

Dragonfury Scotland

Fury of a Highland Dragon

Fury of Shadows

Fury of Denial

Fury of Persuasion

Dragonfury Short Story Collection

Fury of Fate

Fury of Conviction

Dragonfury Series

Fury of Fire

Fury of Ice

Fury of Seduction

Fury of Desire

Fury of Obsession

Fury of Surrender

Circle of Seven Series

Knight Awakened

Knight Avenged

Warriors of the Realm Series

Warrior's Revenge

ABOUT THE AUTHOR

Coreene Callahan is the bestselling author of the Dragonfury Novels and Circle of Seven Series, in which she combines her love of romance and adventure with her passion for history. After graduating with honors in psychology and taking a detour to work in interior design, Coreene finally returned to her first love: writing. Her debut novel, *Fury of Fire* was a finalist in the New Jersey Romance Writers Golden Leaf Contest in two categories: Best First Book and Best Paranormal. She lives in Canada with her family, a spirited Anatolian Shepard, and her wild imaginary world.